Edited by: Partners In Crime Book Services
Cover design by: Rebecca Poole
Formatting by: Rebecca Poole

SPIDER'S AWAKENING

TL SHIVELY

CHAPTER 1

CLANG!
CLANK!

The swords clashed and sparks flew, hitting the walls of the temple as Calista, the daughter of Ares and Arachne, battled her cousin Discord. It was supposed to be training. Of course, Calista learned long ago that her cousins cared nothing for training; they used these "trainings" as a way to get back at her for slights they felt she had done to them, and Discord was the worst.

What had she done to them?

KLUNK!
CLANG!

She refused to cower from their bullying and would stand up to them even if it meant she ended up sporting a bruise or two. It didn't help that Zeus seemed to favor her as well, which wasn't as impressive as one would think. It wasn't like he would stand up for her or protect her from her father's wrath, although he did take pity on her and give her a best friend.

Discord and Strife still haven't forgiven her for that small act of kindness, and Ares was always making sure to bring that up. He seemed to enjoy creating animosity between them, never letting Calista forget that he favored Discord and Strife over her.

THUD!

She landed on her ass as Discord landed a well placed hit and sneered down at her with her sword raised for the killing blow. Not that Discord could truly kill her, they were both goddesses after all and no mere sword could kill them. Discord loved to humiliate her with the knowledge that she had bested her.

The blow never came.

The room lit up in red as Ares entered, sneering down at Calista still on the ground. "I see nothing has changed, still weak as ever, daughter." He never called her by name, just daughter. Nor did he say it in a loving manner, rather he always said it with disgust in his voice. She believed, as many others did, that it was the fact she had Zeus' favor that kept him from doing anything to get rid of her. She knew her father hated her, she just never knew why.

Discord sneered as she re-sheathed her blade then shimmered right next to Ares, her eyes simpering up at him in adoration. "She will never be the daughter you deserve, Lord Ares."

While most of the gods and goddesses liked to wear the white robes with either golden accessories or other colored materials, Ares walked around in black leather trousers and vest adorned with silver, mean-looking spikes and other deadly looking adornments. Discord and Strife, of course, had to emulate their mentor and wear outfits that complimented Ares.

Calista on the other hand chose to go the brown leather route, she refused to wear the white robes of the others but neither did she care to mimic the two before her. Discord, with her sycophant obsession with Ares, made it hard for Calista to contain an eye roll, something her father was quick to notice.

"Have something to say, daughter?" His eyes narrowed on her and her small act of rebellion, something he couldn't let go unchallenged. He wanted her to be subservient to him in all aspects.

She loved to deny him that. She looked up at him, holding her head high. "Nothing, Lord Ares." While he only called her daughter, he refused to let her call him Father.

"I didn't think so." Ares turned from her then, as if she was no longer a concern. Which she knew was exactly what he meant. "Discord, I have something I want you to do."

Discord was practically floating on air at his words. "Anything for you, Lord Ares."

Calista wanted to puke as she watched the exchange.

"You could learn a lot from Discord, daughter." Ares sneered at her but she said nothing. Years of her father's contempt for her taught her to speak little when in his presence, which she kept as minimal as possible. Ares stopped and turned his gaze directly onto her, his eyes narrowing at her. How she hated him, how she longed to be free of him. If only it were that easy. "What are you still doing here?" His words were full of contempt.

She knew better than to point out to him about his own rule of her never leaving without his permission, another painful lesson she refused to repeat. So rather than point out the duplicity of his words, she just shimmered out, but not before she saw the satisfaction in Discord's eyes.

The water crashed against the stone below with such force she wondered how the cliff could withstand it without breaking. A gentle brush against her cheek had her smiling at her companion, her constant companion.

She lifted a finger to rub Scratch on the top of his head. "Hey there little guy, wondered when you would show yourself. Were you out playing with your friends during my beatdown with Discord?" She kissed his head. He wasn't allowed in Ares temple, another reason Calista stayed away from there as much as she could.

A not so common spider who befriended her as a child; with her mother being Arachne it shouldn't have been surprising that she took to the eight legged outcasts. Just like her, they were very misunderstood. Such gentle creatures who had so many benefits, benefits everyone wanted to enjoy as long as they stayed in the shadows.

Discord and Strife had killed Scratch when they saw how close Calista had become to him. Her grandfather found her with silent tears as she mourned the loss of her only friend. With one touch Zeus had brought the little guy back to life and granted him immortality.

The only act of kindness Zeus bestowed upon her, but it was enough to give the other gods and goddesses who hadn't already hated her their reason. To them, that act meant she had the favor of Zeus, something they all wanted but never realized how little it actually meant. Zeus was the epitome of what it meant to be a god, he only acted if it either amused him or if it affected him in any way.

Since that day, Scratch never left her side for long, and no one dared try to kill the little guy either. They feared incurring the wrath of Zeus. Discord and Strife were careful in their tormenting of her after that. Of course, there were others that weren't so lucky, but Calista tried to not think of the very few friends she had made over the years, human mainly, that had fatal "accidents" befall them.

Scratch wasn't your common, everyday spider; brown and hairy, he fit into Calista's palm with big green eyes. He was also her best friend and only protector in this land. The reason he was banished from Ares' temples was due to him attempting to protect her from her father's wrath. Ares had returned defeated from battle and as usual, had decided to take it out on Calista. This time Scratch leapt at the war god to protect his mistress. Ares was so angered that he shot an energy bolt at the Spider, grinning with malice at the charred heap of hair.

Ares wasn't grinning when Scratch pushed up on his eight hairy legs and shook the black soot off him. Whether it was the fact the spider survived his wrath or the fact that Calista now had a champion, she didn't know, but Ares forbade the spider in his temples. So, now Scratch always waited for her whenever she was summoned to Ares' Temple.

Friends weren't something she was allowed to have, gods and goddesses didn't understand the concept of friends. Mortals were only valuable if they amused them or if they were of use to them. And if it suited them they would turn on you, she discovered that at a very young age. Apollo may make the mortal girls and many of the Minor goddesses swoon, but Calista had his number. He was a ruthless, out for himself weasel.

Once, long ago, Calista was one of those doe eyed girls fawning over the golden child. So hungered for any attention, she believed Apollo when he implied a fondness for her. It was almost too late when she discovered Discord and Strife had made a bet with Apollo that he couldn't trick her into taking away Scratch's immortality. When it came to challenges of any kind, the gods and goddesses of Greece refused to lose.

Apollo had tricked her into taking Scratch down to Tartarus, speaking of a fountain deep down in the bowels of Tartarus that would give Scratch the ability to speak. While she could communicate with Scratch, Apollo had attempted to talk to Scratch, finding out that he didn't have the same ability. Apollo had seemed so forlorn when he couldn't communicate with the spider that it made Calista want to make it possible. So promising Apollo that she would make his wish come true, she picked up Scratch tenderly and shimmered out, intending to go to this fountain. The only thought was of having a friend that could share her love of spiders, after all, creatures aren't as frightening if only they were able to communicate.

The only thing that had saved her was the fact that she forgot the tablet on which Apollo had etched the location of the fountain. Shimmering quickly back, she stared in horror at the sight in front of her. Apollo, Discord and Strife were there, lifting their goblets in a toast as they laughed loudly and speaking of how crushed she would be when she realized the fountain had nothing to do with giving Scratch the ability to speak.

It was Discord's words that had her seeing red. "I wish I could be down there to see the horror on the face of the blond twit when she realizes the fountain actually takes away immortality." Her laughter had Calista's teeth clenching.

But it was Apollo's words that sent Calista over the edge as he raised his goblet to his lips. "Not only that, but that gruesome creature will wither right in front of her." He grinned as he took another drink. "How she could think I would want to communicate with such a disgusting thing is beyond me, she only has herself to blame."

That day they learned of the true power Calista carried within her, a power Ares had always refused to allow her to show. A power that had all three of them running away in terror and also that kept Apollo away from her since. Discord and Strife claimed she made them see hallucinations while Apollo stayed silent about that night.

From that day forward, she was known as the Goddess of Insanity, a title she truly didn't care for and one that put her on the Goddess Lyssa's bad side, the true Greek Goddess of Insanity. She still had no idea what she had done or even how she had done it, although it doesn't matter since that was the one and only time her powers showed themselves.

"What are you doing so far from home?"

"Alastor." Calista spoke without turning to greet the god. Alastor was one who enjoyed her company, or so he said. She rarely trusted the word of a god or a goddess anymore. Her blond hair flowed behind her in the wind, which would look epic if Aeolus hadn't decided to make the wind change directions so that her hair ended slapping across her face. She tried swiping it with an angry hand but Aeolus wasn't done playing around and, with a growl, she flopped backward. "Do you understand someone wanting some space?"

"Not really." Alastor walked over and sat next to her, his legs dangling over the edge of the cliff. "Why would someone want space? There is space everywhere."

Calista stared up into the sky above, hoping if she ignored him, he would leave. Most of the gods and goddesses either ignored her or delighted in tormenting her. Then there was Alastor.

"Family quabbles again?"

"Don't you mean squabbles?" Calista watched Scratch who was walking on top of her but keeping one of his many eyes on Alastor, the little guy didn't trust Alastor any more than Calitsta did.

"Nope. Quabbles." Alastor sat there, waiting for her answer.

She gave a deep sigh. "Alastor, there isn't a god or goddess or even mortal in all of Greece that doesn't know of Ares' hatred of me." Her mother may not hate her but she never cared for her either. Actually, her mother acted as if she didn't exist.

"Funny." Alastor spoke, staring out at the sea. Calista waited to see if he would explain what he meant but after a few moments of silence she prompted him.

"What is funny?"

Alastor looked at her then. "Thought you wanted space?"

She really wanted to strangle him and if she actually

thought it would work, she would give it a try to see if it actually shut him up. "Either say what you want or leave me in peace, old man." She growled. If she had dared to call any of the other gods 'old man', they would have been ready to toss her into Hephaestus' forges.

"I am the God of Family Feuds."

Calista nodded, she already knew this. "And I am sure you get much enjoyment from my family."

"That is just it, I get nothing from the feud between you and Ares or even Arachne." He looked at her with a tilt to his head. "Wonder why that is."

Calista snorted. "Not bloody enough for you?"

Alastor paused then shook his head slowly. "That isn't it, I love any feud."

Calista stood not in the mood for riddles anymore. "Well, I don't know what to tell you. I have no desire to examine why my family feud has no thrill for you, I have no desire to even think about it at all." With that said, she shimmered away.

CHAPTER 2

Calista found herself on one of the many cliffs that made up the mountain base of Mount Olympus, looking out over the landscape of Greece after her talk with Alastor. Well, if you wanted to call it a talk. Everyone considered him crazy and there were times Calista agreed. That wasn't the first time he had made remarks on her family, always implying that there was something off about her family and even though he never mentioned her name. she wondered if that was what he was implying.

While other gods and goddesses had temples, that was one of many rights Ares refused her. With no official title nor power, she wasn't really the goddess of anything, so when it came down to it, she was the goddess of nothing. She had nowhere to call home, so there wasn't a place in Greece that she wasn't familiar with.

The caves on the island of Ithaca where the Siren was imprisoned; when Apollo was playing her, he had taken her there. He stood in front of the Siren's cave with that cocky grin of his, telling her how one day the Siren appeared with the weird markings on the cave.

Now the Siren sang from the confines of the cave where she could do no harm. Apollo's words, not hers.

She was familiar with the forges of Hephaestus as she had hidden there a time or two as well. Like her, Hephaestus was shunned by those he called family but unlike her, he at least had a title and a place to call home in his forges. A place he would let her visit when she needed an escape.

A movement to her left had her looking and there were several spiders peeking around some rocks. Whenever she was sad or upset they always seemed to come to her.

She smiled at them, reaching down to pet them gently. Her softness was saved for the spiders, for others, they got exactly what they created. A hard, callous and cynical goddess. She used to yearn for a family that would love and cherish her, but realized as she got older it was foolish. So, she became indifferent to protect herself.

"Well if it isn't the unknown goddess."

There was only one other that she hated more than Discord.

"Strife." She spoke his name with no emotion, nor did she look around to acknowledge him.

The wiry little dark-haired minor god who was a bane to her well-being started prancing around her. How she longed to knock him off the cliff, not that it would do any good. Can't kill a god and all that. "You seem to be upset, I wonder what would make a goddess who isn't even a goddess sad?" His voice dripped with false concern, spoken in such an octave that no male should ever be able to achieve. Not that she thought of Strife as a male, more like an insignificant bug on the wall.

She then looked at him, inside enjoying the flinch while outside showing no emotion at all. "I have no feelings Strife, I thought you knew that."

He tilted his head from side to side as he watched her, a smile forming. That smile bore nothing but ill will towards her, of that she was sure. "Is that so?" He moved with great exaggeration around her, she resisted the urge to watch him. Instead, staring away as if she cared nothing for what he was about to do. "In that case, you won't care when I do this." With those words, she heard the cry of the gentle blue spider that had come to comfort her.

She was glad she hadn't been watching, she didn't think she would have been able to hide the pain his actions caused. By the time Strife moved around to stare into her eyes, they were back to the emotionless orbs that were her armor. Thankfully the little brown one that was blue's companion scurried off before Strife could test her yet again.

"Your only friends, and yet you care nothing when they are squashed like the insects they are." How she hated his voice. "You truly don't have any emotions do you?"

"Spiders aren't insects, Strife," she told him coldly.

"So?" He shrugged.

"They are part of the arachnid family, along with scorpions and many other deadly creatures. They are also very loyal and take death seriously," she told him, staring at him, enjoying how he seemed to grow uncomfortable under her hard stare. "If I were you, I would be cautious."

Strife snorted. "As if any insect could harm a god."

"I guess you never heard the story of the Scorpion and the God of Parlay."

"Who?"

"Exactly." With those cold words, Calista shimmered out, again. She hoped she gave Strife nightmares for the rest of his eternal life even if it meant more grief for her. Not like she wasn't used to it.

Calista leaned against a tree in a forest farthest from Athens, where her father's temple resided. Avoiding her father also meant avoiding Corinth as well. Aphrodite's temple was there, which meant her father could be as well. This forest bordered a cliff over the ocean, as far from everyone and everywhere that she could find.

It felt as if she spent her whole life running. It had been days since Strife had murdered Blue, when she was sure he had left, she went back and buried her little friend. No tears fell while she buried Blue; she never cried anymore. Tears were nothing more than weapons for her enemies and that is exactly what her family was. Scratch, on the other hand, he cried as they stood there by the grave.

That was then and this was now, Scratch was perched in his favorite spot on her shoulder as they both stared out over the water's surface. Whenever she had felt as if her life was spiraling out of control, she found the ocean a calming influence. Which was odd considering Ares had a favorite game that he liked to play whenever he was bored. Imprisoning her in a watery grave, locked in a casket with chains that only he could free her from. Being a goddess, she couldn't die, but the memory of those times all alone at the bottom of the sea and not being able to move for days, months, and once Ares had forgotten her for several years. Those times had haunted her and given her a healthy dose of fear of the water, not that she would admit it.

That would give them more power than they already had over her.

Leaning against the tree, she slid down until she sat on the ground, her head back against the tree and her arms around her knees. She knew she couldn't hide out here forever, Ares would find her sooner or later, when he grew bored and realized she wasn't around to intimidate.

"Well hello there, luv."

Calista opened her eyes at the slow drawl, staring

at the pair of obsidian eyes that grinned down at her. A male dressed in all black leather except for his cotton shirt under his black leather cloak that hung all the way down to his leather boots. His clothes screamed pirate, he even had a sword sheathed at his waist whose handle was made of silver and molded into an intricate design. Not bad looking with those dark looks and a smile that she was sure got his way with many of the ladies. Too bad she wasn't like those ladies.

"Far from the ports, aren't you, pirate?"

The swashbuckling, dark-haired pirate held his hand to his chest with widened eyes and a mocking grin. "Pirate? Now, what would have such a petite little morsel such as yourself calling me a pirate?"

"Not amused, maybe you should go find some twit in the village to charm. I am sure your smile and charming ways will work there. Not here." She went back to staring up in the sky. trying to ignore him. She really didn't need his type of complication in her life.

"Not dashing enough for ya?" His voice spoke of an accent that surely wasn't from around here, but if she was honest with herself, she would have to admit she liked it. "Would I look more appealing with maybe a hook?"

Her head turned quickly to stare up at him with wide eyes. "Why in Hades would that be more appealing?"

He shrugged. "Some ladies like that kind of thing."

"Mutilation? If that is the crowd you hang with,

you might want to rethink your choices." She shook her head. "And I thought I lived in a viper pit."

He chuckled before sitting down next to her on the ground, crossing his legs. "Do you mind?" he asked as she stared at him incredulously.

"Would it matter?" She arched a brow at him.

He shrugged and pulled out his flask, taking a drink before he continued, "Yes, you could call me a pirate of sorts. If you wanted to." He winked at her. "But there is much more to me than my swashbuckling ways."

"Let me guess, you want to take me to your ship and show me." Her tone was droll but it seemed to roll right off that ego of his.

"You do like to move fast, luv, but please slow down, I'm not that kind of man." He grinned, taking another swig from his flask as he watched her with what looked like actual enjoyment. She wondered if this was one of Strife's tricks, but dismissed that completely. That fool couldn't pull off anything this debonair even with Discord coaching him. Apollo? Now that was a possibility, even if he usually kept his distance. She wouldn't put it past him.

She was sure he was expecting her to ask him what type of man he was but refused to give in and let him boast of himself. Most definitely Apollo. "I would ask if you are slumming it but then again, slumming is a pirate's life."

He looked taken back by her words, Apollo seriously couldn't expect her to truly fall for this, could he? She had to admit she didn't get any god or goddess vibes from him, but he was no mere mortal. That she was sure of.

"Such poisonous words from such sweet lips, someone has done a number on you, luv." The pirate took yet another long swig from his flask.

"You could say that." She nodded. "And if you were smart, you would stay far away … pirate." If this wasn't Apollo, then she thought it only fair to try to warn him.

He gave her a roguish grin. "Never been accused of that, luv, guess you'll just have to suck it up and get used to having a pirate around."

She barely refrained from rolling her eyes. Years of practice helped her to hide her emotions.

"Your funeral," she told him as she closed her eyes again, her head back, leaning on the tree and ignoring him yet again. She was here first, if he wanted to endanger his life that was on him. The wind picked up around them and she could hear laughter on the wind. Aeolus seemed to find something about this amusing. She cracked open one eye and realized the pirate was still sitting there watching her.

"I'm still here, luvs." He had the roguish grin down for sure.

It was time she put an end to this. "Look, Apollo, this has been fun and all, not really." She looked over at him and gave him a smirk. "Go play your games elsewhere." With that, she shimmered away, leaving Apollo there in his pirate finery.

CHAPTER 3

Ares' temple was empty except for Discord, who was draped across the war god's throne of bones that adorned the dais. There wasn't an eye roll hard enough. Discord sneered when she saw her walking across the floor.

"The worthless goddess returns." She scoffed. Calista didn't even acknowledge her presence, just walked past her to head to her room but Discord's next words had her stopping. "Lord Ares has some important business to attend to with Apollo, he wanted me to make sure you didn't slack in your training."

Calista turned to stare at Discord. "Ares is out with Apollo?"

"Having hearing problems?" Discord sneered at her. "That is what I said."

"When did they leave?"

Discord looked over at her. "Why does it matter?"

"Because it does. When did they leave?" Calista stared at Discord, her gaze hard. Discord's eyes narrowed at her.

"Not that it is any business of yours, but they left

hours ago, now make sure you don't make me wait too long or else I will make your training more humiliating than normal." Discord shimmered out in a cloud of black, her voice irritated. She would be even more so if she truly expected Calista to listen to her.

She had a pirate to locate.

The pirate wasn't hard to locate, but then again she had this weird feeling he wanted her to find him. There he was in a tavern in Delphi chatting up a barmaid with that smile and that pirate brogue of his. She wasn't sure what made her do it but she gave Scratch a wink. The scream of terror from the barmaid upon seeing Scratch on the table before she ran from the table brought a smirk to her face.

"Guess you do have a bit of your father in you?"

She frowned at him. "No need for insults, pirate."

He chuckled. "Wasn't an insult, I think highly of your father."

That stopped her. "Of Ares?" She wasn't used to hearing that unless it was from a warlord or a general in one of his many armies. Not from a pirate.

He scoffed. "Not that buffoon, your real father."

Now he truly had her attention. "Excuse me?"

There was that roguish grin again. At this rate, she was going to end up with her eyes in the back of her head. Damn pirate was making her roll her eyes too much. "Do I perhaps have the Spider's attention?"

"Spider?" She frowned.

He gave a pointed look at Scratch, who was watching him intently. Scratch was protective of his mistress, considering she ended up being the proverbial punching bag to many around here. She smiled at Scratch's thoughts on the pirate, her little baby was intrigued by the stranger. Silently she agreed with him although he irritated as much as intrigued her. Which wasn't the best for his health, though he didn't seem to care.

She gave a shrug. "My mother is Arachne," she stated.

"Are you sure about that?" The pirate took a swig from his goblet that looked as if it had been through many bar fights. It probably had. This bar was well known for their brawls.

The barmaid sashayed back over giving Calista the stink eye. "Would you like a drink?" she asked sweetly but her eyes were practically shooting daggers at her.

Calista tilted her head and looked up at the red, mussy haired barmaid and gave a smile as if she wasn't being stared at like an unwanted interloper. If the mortal could actually intimidate her, she had no idea who she was dealing with. "I won't be here long enough for a drink."

"Good." The barmaid then dismissed her and turned towards the pirate. "Is there anything else I can get you, handsome?"

The pirate raised a dark brow. "Privacy is all we need, luv."

Calista sighed. She had been through enough jealous harpies to know something was going to end up happening, something not in her favor. Turned out she was correct. The barmaid straightened up quickly, her eyes full of anger at being rebuked whether it was a gentle one or not. So when the two metal goblets full of ale on her tray ended up in Calista's lap, she wasn't surprised.

"Oh, I'm soooo sorry." The fake apologetic voice with the snide smile was the final draw.

With a smile that had the barmaid perplexed, she waved a hand and her leather breeches were no longer wet. It was as if it never happened. She enjoyed the widening eyes of the female as she realized she had just poured her drinks over a goddess. The female quickly disappeared, she couldn't get behind the bar fast enough. A scream and the clanging sound of the tray hitting the floor could be heard from the other room the barmaid had disappeared to.

"*Spider!*"

Calista smiled, ignoring the pirate's sharp rebuke, petting Scratch on his head, after he scurried up her leg to sit on her shoulder.

"You already had her freaked out with your little magic trick, did you really have to sic your little pet on the poor lass?"

Her smile gone, she stared right at him. "Poor lass? You may not have seen it, but I know her kind and trust me, she deserved so much more."

The pirate shook his head at her. "You can't judge everyone on the fools who have tormented you your whole life."

She snorted. "Says who?"

He sighed. "Such a cynical heart hidden beneath such beauty."

She frowned. "You are a pirate, so what do you care? You pillage and pilfer wherever you go and yet you think to lecture me?"

He raised a brow. "Making assumptions, luv? You don't know me to say such things but we can always remedy that." He grinned at her.

"You know what? Nevermind." Calista stood up. "I thought you might actually have something to say that might be of interest to me, but all you have done is waste my time. I'll leave you to the little twit who's waiting for me to leave."

She turned to leave but he reached out and snagged her arm in his grip. She didn't look at him, just at his hand, but he still held firm. What was up with this male? She had never had anyone try this hard to have anything to do with her, not unless there was an ulterior motive.

"I have no desire to spend any more time than necessary with the overzealous serving maid." His voice was smooth but firm.

Still her gaze never wavered from his grasp. "Then I suggest you find someone else, I'm not good for anyone's well-being." That was no lie, if someone actually had good intentions with her, then Ares would cure them of that pretty quickly.

"Why? Will the fools who pretend to be your family try to end me?" There was no mockery at her expense in his tone although she could hear a bit of a bitter tone.

She moved her head to look into his eyes, there was amusement there but no sign of the slight bitterness in his voice. He didn't seem to be afraid of the consequences knowing her could incur. Not something she was used to.

"Give me five minutes of your time, luv, what can it hurt? If you want to walk away after that then I'll not stop you." There was that grin again.

She smirked at him. "I can walk away now." With that said, she shimmered from the tavern.

She smiled at Scratch, who shook his head at her. Kissing him softly on his head, she said, "We don't need some scoundrel of a pirate, no matter how devilishly handsome he is. Even if he was genuine, Ares or one of the others would end up chasing him off or worse. I refuse to be responsible for another death."

"Devilishly handsome huh?"

She twirled around to see him standing there, the corners of his eyes crinkled with amusement. Who in the Hades was this guy? "How?"

"You aren't dealing with some run of the mill pirate, luvs, I'm actually a Hunter." He grinned.

"A Hunter? What is that?" Her head tilted as she looked him over.

"Exactly what it says, I hunt down things and sometimes people." He lifted a shoulder as if to say it wasn't a big deal.

"Hunters also kill," her back straightened as her gaze hardened on him. She wondered exactly who had put a bounty on her head, the possibilities were endless.

His brows drew together at her words and it took him a few moments before he responded, "I can promise you I'm not here to kill anyone."

"So why then? You can't seriously expect me to believe that you are looking for me?"

"Why not?" He plucked a blade of grass off the ground and put it into his mouth as he watched her closely. "You think no one would be looking for you?"

Her brow knitted, his words made no sense to her. "But why? Who would want to find me?"

"Your parents."

She blanched and stepped back. "What do you mean?"

"You seriously don't believe that you're the product of Ares and Arachne?" He asked; his tone spoke of disgust.

She blinked at him. "Not like I had any indication I wasn't."

He chuckled. "Maybe the fact that you've more power in one of your little fingers than either of those two could ever hope to have. Why do you think Ares goes out of his way to make you think you're insignificant? He fears you."

She snorted at his words. "You don't know what you are talking about, besides if what you're saying is true, why did my parents give me away?"

"The only way to find the answers is to come with me." He smiled and moved towards her. "You ready to discover who you truly are?"

She stared at his hand but didn't take it. "How do I know I can trust you? I don't even know your name."

"Solen, now we must go before Ares' little snitches decide to go running to him and tell him you aren't playing the puppet to their strings."

She sighed, he was right about that. Whenever she tried to defy Discord or Strife in Ares' absence they would go running to Ares, who would make sure to promptly take his displeasure out on Calista as soon as he returned. But then again, she truly didn't know Solen, although anything had to be better than here. Before she could change her mind, she placed her hand in his.

As soon as their hands touched they disappeared from where they were standing on the land, to deep beneath the surface of the ocean. Her chest tightened as she had flashbacks to Ares' punishments, her breathing started to become ragged in her agitation.

Calm down Calista, you are a goddess. You won't die and I promise you, you won't be a prisoner here.

She looked over at Solen as she heard his voice in her head. She tried to calm her already shaky nerves, not that she would ever admit that to anyone. No weakness! She gave him a nod but refrained from speaking whether via the telepathic link he opened up or verbally, which would have given her a mouthful of water that even for a goddess would have been uncomfortable but not life-threatening.

She followed him through the water, curious where they were going and at the same time doing her best to keep the panic attack to a minimum. The mortals of the world would laugh to hear a goddess having a panic attack because she was in the middle of the ocean with a pirate who wasn't really a pirate. Solen truly intrigued her, but still, she didn't trust him. Growing up with parents like Ares and Arachne taught her no one can be trusted.

A gentle caress on her neck had her realizing that Scratch was still there, she looked at her only friend and saw that over his head was an air bubble. He was immortal after all but even he couldn't breathe under water.

You're welcome, came Solen's telepathic amused words, which she completely ignored.

Solen descended even further down and, fighting the sudden flurry of butterflies in her stomach, she followed suit until her feet touched the bottom of the ocean floor. They moved past the colorful stones and flora all around them. She couldn't contain the smile as a vibrant colored fish came up close to them, very interested in Scratch, who kept swatting at it with one of his hairy little legs. Her little spider found a friend. The fish looked at her as if asking for permission to eat Scratch, she frowned and shook her head so the fish swam away.

Come on little spider, you can play with the fishies later, Solen's telepathic voice spoke once more as he reached his hand out to her but she just gestured that he move forward. He gave a shake of his head, then kept walking forward with her trailing behind him. She walked past a rock formation with some very lovely flowers growing on it. She picked a lovely blue flower from it, enjoying how the long petals swayed in the water.

That isn't a flower.

She frowned at Solen's words then gasped when the flower rose from her hand and swam away. She almost choked on the water that she swallowed when she gasped but with a wave of Solen's hand the water was gone. Solen smiled at her then gestured for her to follow him again.

It's not far, Spider.

She frowned at him calling her Spider. Usually when she was called that it was in a derogatory manner, but he actually sounded friendly.

It felt as if they floated across the ocean floor for only a few more minutes, she couldn't say walk when each time she lifted her foot it was as if she moved several feet forward before her foot once again touched the ocean floor. In front of them Calista could see the change in the water, there was something magical there hidden by a spell of some sort. Solen moved forward and disappeared from her view.

Calista stopped dead still in the water, her body tightened at the thought of moving forward into the unknown. She wasn't sure what was hiding here in the ocean, not far from her home and not sure if she wanted to know.

Who was hiding? Why were they hiding?

Come on, little spider. You're not scared, are you?

She knew it was juvenile, but Solen's words had her moving forward through the invisible barrier. The world around her swirled with brilliant colors as she moved, her body tense as she prepared for what waited on the other side.

CHAPTER 4

Calista wasn't sure what she expected but what she saw had her staring like one of the mortals when they first entered a temple, wide-eyed and looking around in awe. Gone was the water, the air was breathable and the view was breathtaking. More majestic than any temple in Greece, even Mount Olympus itself. There were temples of all sizes and structures, glistening from light that she had no idea where it came from. After all, they were under the sea, no sun. Green grass with cobbled trails so meticulously groomed she was sure every blade of grass was perfect. Aphrodite would be jealous.

As she looked around she realized that this place stretched out far over the sea floor. She wasn't sure of the size but she was sure it rivaled that of Athens. The buildings were all different sizes and shapes, while some looked to be white marble there were many more made of other stones just as beautiful.

A little pop and Scratch jumped from her shoulder to a nearby stone pillar standing at a colorful cobbled street that led to a white stone temple. Colored fabric draped from windows in decoration, whoever resided in that temple was sure to be as beautiful as the structure itself. This turned out to be accurate.

The woman who walked towards them had dark auburn hair that flowed freely around her, her lithe form was welcoming as she held out a petite hand to Solen, who took it and placed a small kiss there. Calista felt a tinge of something but she refused to believe that she could be jealous of a male she wasn't sure she could trust.

"Lady Rowena," Solen spoke with respect.

Rowena, that name meant nothing to Calista and yet when the goddess turned to Calista, she smiled as if they were old friends.

"Calista," her voice spoke of relief and joy, yet Calista still had no idea who she was.

"Do we know each other?" Calista stepped back, feeling better when Scratch jumped from the pillar to her shoulder once again.

Rowena, who had taken a step towards her, stopped and stepped back with a sad smile. Calista almost felt responsible for the sad smile, then she remembered that she hadn't asked to come here, she was brought here. "Unfortunately you don't know me but I do know you."

"How?"

Again that sad smile. "If you would be so kind as to follow me into my home, I will gladly tell you everything I can."

Calista looked to Solen, who nodded as if to tell her

she should follow Rowena. She had a problem with trusting and this was asking a lot of her. Solen winked at her when her brow creased at him.

"You can trust her, Spider, I promise. I'll be around if you need me, just give me a shout." He tapped his head, implying the telepathic link they had established while under the water. "I won't be far."

She felt a bit better at hearing that, then angry that she had. She knew better than to lean on others for anything, it never got her anything but pain. She frowned. "I won't need your help, pirate, I'm capable of taking care of myself."

Solen nodded. "As you wish milady." He gave a mocking bow making sure to do elaborate hand motions which did nothing to improve her mood with him.

Rowena watched with amusement dancing in her eyes as she gave a throaty chuckle. "I promise, no ill will shall befall you while you are here." Rowena turned to Solen, "Tylaos and Malov are waiting for you."

Calista watched Solen depart, leaving her alone with Rowena.

"Follow me, Calista, it's time you knew the truth." Rowena turned and headed towards her temple.

"What truth?" Calista asked as she stood there unmoving.

Rowena's mouth curved into a smile, "only one way to find out." When Calista, whose curiosity was too much even for her, started to follow, Rowena gave a tinkling little laugh. "You have the curiosity of your father."

Calista snorted. "You've never met Ares then."

Rowena's face darkened. "Unfortunately I have." She spoke through stiff lips. "But fortunately he wasn't who I was speaking of."

Calista opened her mouth to ask what she meant, but Rowena shook her head. "All will be revealed in my Seer Pool."

Calista followed her into her temple of pure white marble and stone, colored tapestries adorned the walls and sculptures hung out in alcoves. Unlike the Greek deities, the sculptures weren't of the goddess Calista was following. Rather, there were sculptures of others she hadn't seen before. She stopped at one sculpture, the wind knocked from her at the sight. It was a sculpture of her as a child with Scratch perched upon her shoulder.

Scratch jumped down from her shoulder to sit on the shoulder of the young Calista. He looked up at the face, lifting one of his legs to touch the cheek, then looked back at Calista, letting her know that he approved.

"Yes, that's you, Calista, I've watched over you from afar your whole life," Rowena spoke softly from behind her.

Calista turned to look at Rowena, pressing her lips together, never had anyone wanted anything that reminded them of her. Her own parents never wanted anything to do with her. "Why?"

Rowena motioned towards the middle of the temple where a gorgeous fountain stood. Statues of ocean life seemed to dance in the fountain base while colorful droplets of water fell from above. It seemed the people here loved color. Rowena took a seat on one of the stone benches around the water where images were starting to appear. Calista took a seat on the other bench Rowena motioned to, while looking down into the scene playing out in the water's surface.

"This is how I've watched over you from afar, this is called my Seer Pool. I'm able to see anywhere in the world with this, and anytime," Rowena's voice was soft as she watched the awe on Calista's face with fondness.

Calista stared in fascination as images of Strife and Discord came into view, they were standing on one of the many beaches in Greece, shouting her name angrily. Calista's eyes narrowed at them both, the memory of Strife killing the blue spider still fresh in her mind.

Rowena's next words had Calista looking up at her. "Those two have been very lucky my powers couldn't reach that far...until now, that is."

Rowena gave a sly smile, looking up at Calista she dipped her finger into the water, touching the ground beneath the two. Calista gasped as the ground started pulling them down, no matter how they struggled. They couldn't even shimmer out and she knew they were trying to. The ground swallowed them whole and she looked up at Rowena. "Are they okay?"

Rowena gave her a curious look. "Does it really matter?"

Calista stared back into the water; yes, she hated them both but did she truly want something bad to happen to them? She had been tormented by them her whole life but yet she still felt a twinge of concern for them.

Rowena laughed softly. "Do not worry little one, no harm will come to them even if it's what they deserve. Although I can't guarantee Hades won't try to skin them when they drop in on him and his wife during dinner."

Calista laughed at that. Hades wasn't one for guests, and he hated unannounced ones even worse. Now that she knew their fate, she had other questions. "How does this answer why you were watching me?"

Rowena beamed at her. "Smart and quick-minded, just like your mother." Rowena laughed as Calista opened her mouth to say something about Arachne but shut it remembering Rowena's comment earlier about Ares. "As I said, smart like your mother. Just watch the water, my dear, and learn how the Atlanteans became a cursed pantheon and lost one of their own."

Calista turned towards the water and watched as the scene unfolded in front of her. She saw Ares approaching a couple who were laughing together in the sun on a beach she knew wasn't in Greece, at least nowhere she had seen.

Ares puffed out his chest as the couple turned to

him and smiled, the female rising and holding out her hand. "Hello, you must be Ares. We were told to expect your arrival. I am Malis, the Atlantean Goddess of War, Strategy, and Planning—"

"I know who you are," Ares interrupted her as his gaze moved over her slowly, his interest obvious.

"Yes, well, this is my husband," Malis said as a fair-haired male stepped forward protectively and held out his hand to Ares, who took it grudgingly. "Cael, the God of Trickery and Illusion."

Ares gave him a dismissive look, releasing his hand quickly and turning his attention back to Malis. "I was informed you would be showing me around. After all, our powers do compliment one another." The innuendo was clear and Cael stepped closer to his wife. Malis put a calming hand on his arm.

"I'll show you around our wondrous pantheon, Ares," Malis spoke softly but firmly. Then turning to her husband and mate. "Cael, I'll be okay and will return before long." The love between the two was hard to miss, although Calista knew from experience that Ares cared nothing for love. All he cared about were his wants and it was pretty evident he wanted Malis.

Cael smiled at his mate and wife, kissed her lips then knelt down, ignoring Ares' scoff, and kissed her seemingly flat belly before rising back up. "Take care, my love, you walk with the two most important parts of me." He turned to look at Ares. "Take heed, Greek God of War, that you also walk with the two most important parts of me."

Malis sighed as her mate disappeared and Ares looked smug. She gestured for him to follow her as she walked around Atlantis and showed him the Atlantean Pantheon. Ares kept making snide comments that the temples were too colorful to be taken seriously. "The color of one's temple doesn't signify the power of the god or goddess, only they can do that," was her response to him. As they walked she introduced him to many of the others.

They were coming up on a god who was in front of his temple admiring the drawings of his acolytes speaking to them as he gestured to their work with a look of pride. Malis started to slow as they got closer but Ares placed his hand in the small of her back and pushed her forward past the god and his artistic acolytes.

"I was going to introduce you to Atmos, he is the God of Wisdom and the Arts," Malis protested while looking back but Ares just scoffed and continued to move them forward.

"That pretentious blowhard? What do I care about finger paints and plaster?" Ares sounded as arrogant as always, still guiding them forward until Malis stopped and turned around to face him.

"Pretentious? I know most of the Greek gods and goddesses don't have the flair for the colors as we do, but I do know Aphrodite has been known to spread some color in her temple." Malis stared up at Ares as she spoke, Calista noticed the slight tick in Ares' jaw, a sure tell-tale sign that he was getting agitated.

"Aphrodite? You want to be considered as trivial as her?" Ares could barely contain the contempt in his voice.

Malis stared up at him, her jaw slack and eyes wide. "You consider love trivial?"

"You're the Goddess of War, aren't you?"

"No! And I can't believe you do, wars have been fought over love."

Ares snorted. "Love has its place, but it isn't on the battlefield. Just like finger painting, they all have their places." Ares shrugged, already dismissing the subject. "If they want to create a portrait or bust of me, that I'll allow, but I won't have any peace lovers corrupting my army."

"But without creativity, how could we come up with strategies to win a war with few casualties, or create a more peaceful solution?"

That seemed to catch Ares' attention. "Why would you want a peaceful solution? You are the Goddess of War."

"Because war isn't to the benefit of our people. Can't you see that?" Malis shook her head at him. "War brings death and suffering, it should only be used as a last resort."

Ares looked down at her and lifted her chin with a

finger, looking right into her eyes. "War is everything. You take what you want and let no one stand in your way." He leaned down to kiss her but ended up on the floor writhing in pain with Malis holding her hand over her belly, staring down at him, anger sparkling from her eyes.

"I introduced you to my husband and yet you still attempted to kiss me?" Her energy crackled around her as she glared down at Ares. "You're not welcome in Atlantis any more, Greek God of War."

Ares glared up at her. "I will have you."

Malis snorted at that and, with a loud snapping sound, she sent him back to Greece, then leaned against her mate who had appeared with a frown, his hand moving protectively to her belly. The water became clear once more.

Calista looked at Rowena. "Malis was pregnant?" Rowena nodded and Calista snorted. "Yeah, that sounds like Ares. Refusing to notice anything he doesn't care to acknowledge." Her head shot up. "Ares didn't start a war with Atlantis, did he?"

Rowena gave a small laugh. "Oh he tried, but none of the other Greek gods wanted a war with Atlantis, they might outnumber us but unlike the Greeks, our Pantheon was a bit less chaotic." She laughed. "We have a God of Chaos who grumbles constantly that he would have more fun in Greece."

"So what happened?" Calista asked curiously.

"Ares claimed to have discovered an Oracle that told him of a curse that would send our Pantheon to the bottom of the ocean. Atlanteans would be unable to leave or communicate with the outside world." Rowena looked into the fountain. Calista saw Malis on a bed while Cael held a baby in his arms. "He was told he needed a product of his jealousy, so while Atlantis slept, a traitor snuck into their home and stole their baby. The traitor gave the baby to Ares, who presented the baby to the Oracle."

In the water, Calista watched Ares sneer down at the innocent babe. Then the vision faded and once again the water was clear in the basin. She looked up at Rowena. "What happened?"

"My vision pool has never shown me what happened at the Oracle. The only reason we know what transpired is because Ares wanted us to know. He had taken a child to give to the Oracle thinking they wanted a sacrifice. He was wrong." Rowena smiled at Calista who was beginning to understand. "The Oracle told Ares that in order for the curse to work, he would have to keep the child safe and far from the ocean. The child could never enter Atlantis. For the moment she did, the curse would be broken."

"Me?"

Rowena nodded. "Welcome home, daughter of Malis and Cael."

CHAPTER 5

Calista followed Rowena to the courtyard in Rowena's temple. It was situated in the center of the temple with a gorgeous landscape that gave one the feeling of pure contentment and peace. Columns held up the second floor that surrounded the courtyard, beautiful white marble columns with intricate etchings that wrapped around.

"How do I know what you're telling me is the truth?" Calista forced herself to ask. While the idea of Ares and Arachne not being her parents was more than appealing, she was used to betrayal and deceit. It was strange for her to accept what Rowena shared.

Rowena gave Calista a half smile. "I can understand your hesitation. Your life wasn't the easiest growing up in Greece under the thumb of Ares." Moving lithely around the flora and statues in her garden, Rowena placed her hands on the back of a stone bench, turning to look at Calista. "I just ask you to give us a chance, to show you this is your home and the Atlanteans are your people."

Calista nodded, still leary but truly curious as well,

"When do I get to meet the other Atlanteans?"

"Soon," Rowena promised, "but there was one re-union I thought should be more private." With that serene smile of hers, she disappeared into one of the many doorways around the courtyard, leaving Calista standing there looking around while chewing on her bottom lip.

It wasn't long before Calista discovered what Rowena had meant.

"Calista?" A tentative voice came from behind her.

Turning around, she knew she was looking at her parents, her true parents, even without the visions from Rowena's pool. Looking at her mother she felt as if she was looking into a mirror, the resemblance was so pronounced, and Calista smiled as she realized she had her father's eyes.

Although very unsure of what to do, after all growing up with Ares and Arachne, she was used to no affection. She was sure she had forgotten how to hug.

But her parents hadn't; they rushed forward and wrapped her in their arms.

"My baby," Malis crooned as she squeezed her tightly.

"My loves," Cael's soft-spoken voice surrounded them both as a loving cocoon.

How long they stood like that, Calista didn't know, but for the first time in her life she felt the love of a parent's embrace. She flinched when they had approached her at first but when all they did was embrace her, she wrapped her arms around them both. Tears flowed down her cheek unchecked, never had she been allowed to release them without being punished for being weak.

It was many hours later that they had finally stopped crying and hugging, Calista was sitting with her parents on one of the majestic marble benches in Rowena's court-yard. They told her about life under the water in Atlantis after being cursed and she told them of her life with Ares and Arachne. Several times she had to pause as Cael would curse out and threaten to visit Ares personally.

Had she ever had anyone in Greece come to her defense in such a way?

Malis put her hand on Cael's arm. "We can have a chat with the Greeks at a later date, now I would like to enjoy having our daughter home."

Cael gave her a boyish grin. "As always, my life, you are right." He kissed her softly then smiled at Calista. "Are you ready to meet the rest of your family?"

Calista smiled at the streak of blue that adorned her hair, a homecoming gift from Atmos, who seemed genuinely pleased to see her. Salis, the God of Agriculture and Inspiration, bowed to her when they were introduced. She couldn't stop herself from comparing Atlantis to

Greece and Greece was losing. Surely this place couldn't be this perfect?

Her mother laughed when she voiced her thoughts out loud. "We would never be as bold to boast such a fallacy."

"I don't know, I think perfect is the perfect word for us." Cael grinned down at his wife, who rolled her eyes at him.

"Some of us aren't as vain as others." She pushed at him, laughing. "Gods are no different than mortals when it comes to flaws."

"Actually, they can be worse."

Calista turned to see a dark-haired couple smiling at her. The male stood well over a foot and a half above the female, his arm draped over her shoulder affectionately. His robes were a golden yellow with a shiny gold rope belted around his waist with golden adornments hanging down. Hers were a light blue with silver circle adornments clasped on her shoulders.

"Mother, father." Malis smiled at them and then turned to Calista. "Your granddaughter is home. Calista, your grandparents, Tylaos and Malov. Not only are they the rulers of our home, but your grandfather Tylaos is our God of Time and Technology, while your grandmother Malov is the Goddess of Life and Death."

Malov moved forward and embraced Calista, then jumped back when Scratch peeked out from beneath her hair. She held her breath worried about her family's reaction to her best friend. A worry that was unfounded as Malov smiled down at Scratch as she reached out her hand and scratched his head. If he had been a cat, he would have purred.

"Hello, granddaughter, hello, Scratch." Malov gave a genuine smile.

"You know his name?" Calista's brow furrowed.

Malov laughed. "My dear, we've watched you grow from Rowena's pool."

"Of course we would know about your friend." Tylaos smiled at her.

"We gods and goddesses are worse than humans with our faults because, unlike the humans, we have powers and even the greatest of us have been known to abuse it when it has suited us," Malov explained. "Unfortunately, the Greeks aren't the only ones who fall from grace."

Tylaos kissed her on her head. "But none can look as beautiful as you, my love."

Malov laughed and slapped at him before smiling once again at Calista. "Welcome home granddaughter, we are so happy to finally have you back where you belong. Explore your home and get acquainted with everyone, we will see you at the feast tonight."

With a smile, they both shimmered from sight.

Calista ended up with a piece of wheat in her hair

from Salis, the God of Agriculture and Inspiration, who said she was a sign of a good harvest. She never thought about a harvest on the bottom of the ocean floor but then again, she never thought of a whole pantheon living here either. Her Aunt Brine was petite but very kind as she hugged her and introduced her to her disciples.

When they walked away, Calista looked at her mother. "There are humans that live here as well?"

"Of course," Her mother smiled at her. "When Atlantis was cursed, they not only cursed us, they cursed all those that worshiped us. They have lived here with us on the ocean floor where we have taken care of them and they've worked alongside us."

Would the Greeks have done that? Maybe a few, but most of them only cared for themselves. Calista felt a slow-burning anger growing deep inside, anger at Ares for not only taking her from her family but the abuse she suffered at his hands. Her mother's calming hand on her shoulder had her looking up in shock.

"This is a day of celebration, my daughter, not of anger and vengeance."

How did her mother know her so well? Could she read minds?

Malis laughed. "You are so like your father Calista, your thoughts are written all over your face, but no fear, I'll always be here to be the calm to both your storms." With that, she gave Calista a gentle squeeze.

She didn't get to meet Stratos, as he was in his

chambers in consultation. When she asked who with, Cael shrugged. "Stratos doesn't answer to anyone."

"But everyone has to answer to someone." Calista was confused.

Malis smiled at her daughter. "Stratos is the God of Judgment and Justice, he is neutral in all things. His decree is final, and so he answers to no one."

Calista opened her mouth to ask another question but decided against it and closed it. Her father chuckled and ruffled her hair.

"You'll get used to it, my daughter, even if you don't understand it." She loved his boyish grin already and could see why her mother had fallen for him. When he called her his daughter it was nothing like when Ares called her daughter, this was filled with love and affection.

All the temples she had seen were colorful and different, even the marble and stone they were made out of were different from each other. Brine's she was told were made out of coral. She loved the non-uniformity of Atlantis.

As they walked, Calista noticed a temple off to the side; the lawn was unkempt and grown over. Dead plants and trees adorned not only the land around the temple but the temple itself. No color for the structure that looked like no marble or stone she had ever seen and it was completely black.

"Is that the counterpart to Hades?"

Her father's eyes darkened as he looked at the temple but it was her mother who answered her.

"No, here in Atlantis we don't fear death and don't look upon it as ugly. Your grandmother is the Goddess of Life and Death and she is celebrated."

"That is the temple of a traitor, the very one who carried you from our home to Ares," Cael growled as his hands balled into fists. Malis placed a hand on his arm but Calista saw the tightening of her face as well.

"Why don't you tear down the temple? Why keep that reminder?"

Her mother smiled at her. "It is a reminder that not all things are as they seem and to always be prepared for the unseen."

"Blah, blah, blah!" Calista jerked around to see three guys standing there grinning like fools. One was Solen, and she felt a twinge of something upon seeing him but she refused to acknowledge it. The other two resembled each other with their fair looks and bright blue eyes. No robes for these two, they wore tight green leather breeches and boots. Bare chested unless you count the leather straps that criss crossed with silver breast plates adorned with dragons.

Her father threw back his head and laughed. "Ahhh, the troublesome duo have arrived to meet our daughter."

"Troublesome?" one of the males said, holding his hand to his heart. "I'm hurt that you would say such a thing, at least when you say it make sure to acknowledge that we are also the best looking in this Pantheon."

Solen snorted and shook his head. "Calista, these are the dragon brothers." His head inclined to the one on his left, whose light brown hair fell in curls around his very handsome face. "This one is Rikar and the other one is his brother, Draken."

"Dragons?"

"Water dragons at that." The one called Draken grinned and moved forward, lifting Calista's hand while he placed a gentle kiss on the back. "Sons of Poseidon, our father is a crafty devil who loves adventure."

Calista didn't miss the frown on Solen's face but she didn't acknowledge it. Smiling at the brothers, she said, "You guys were in Atlantis when it was cursed? Poseidon allowed that?" She knew Greek gods weren't the best parents, but their ego wouldn't let their own children be cursed, would it?

Rikar shrugged. "The old man has had some issues with some of our life choices."

"Life choices?"

Draken placed his arm around Calista's shoulder and grinned. There was that frown on Solen's face again. "Let's just say we aren't daddy's favorites and leave it at that." He had a grin that screamed trouble but for some reason, it made her smile, too.

"How about we show your daughter around and tell her a bit about Atlantis?" Rikar grinned at Malis and Cael, who seemed to be enjoying the show as well from the grins on their faces.

Cael looked at Rikar, grin gone. "Just remember she's our daughter and if anything you do upsets her, I'll be having dragon throw rugs."

Calista's eyes widened at her father's words, torn between enjoying the fact she had someone willing to defend her like that and the fear of a brawl starting on her first day home. Her mother laughed and kissed her cheek.

"Ignore them, Cali." When Calista frowned at the nickname her mother had given her, her mother looked concerned. "If you don't like me calling you Cali, I can just call you Calista."

"No, no, it's all right." Calista felt embarrassed. "I have never had a nickname, unless it was an insult." She shrugged. "I like it."

"Then I shall continue to call you Cali." Her mother smiled. "But as I was saying, you can ignore them. Your father and those two always poke at one another but you'll discover they're best of friends."

Rikar snorted. "What best friend threatens to use you for a throw rug?"

Malis raised an eyebrow at him. "What best friend turns one's home into a water bomb minefield full of lobsters and crabs?"

"You know, it's getting late and if we want to show little Cali around all the secrets of Atlantis, we should really get moving." His brother placed his hand under her elbow and pulled her with him.

"Don't think you're leaving me out." Solen appeared on the other side of Calista and winked at her.

Rikar hollered back as they walked away, "For the record, you weren't supposed to arrive home before Cael."

Calista laughed as they dragged her with them, running through the temples and jumping over boulders and stone benches.

CHAPTER 6

Caves?" Calista frowned, pulling back with a suspicious look.

All three of the males stopped and looked at her with a frown. "What's wrong with caves?"

"You are telling me the treasures of Atlantis are in a cave?" She didn't mean to sound so distrusting but she was. She had been fooled by a pretty smile before and she wasn't about to be again.

Draken walked towards her, but Solen put up his hand. Draken nodded and he and Rikar disappeared deeper into the cave.

Solen walked over to her. "What's wrong, luv, thought you wanted to see the treasures of Atlantis?"

She crossed her arms and glared up at him. "I have been fooled by a pretty face before, I won't be fooled again."

Solen grinned down at her, why did the idiot have to be taller than she?

"Pretty face huh? I would have rather been described as dashing or roguish, but I will take pretty." He sighed when she didn't move but simply stared at him. "Spider, do you really think your parents would go through the lengths they did to get you home only to try to harm you?"

Calista pointed into the cave. "One, those aren't my parents, and two, aren't you forgetting about the family I grew up with?"

Solen slipped his arm around her with that smile of his. "I'll be by your side the whole time and I promise you that those two are completely harmless. They may be full of themselves most of the time and the other half not as serious as they should be, but they're not only keepers of Atlantis' secrets and history but trusted warriors in your mother's army." He looked down at her. "Come on, give them a chance."

Calista narrowed her eyes at him, trying to hold back the smile that threatened to break through. "Fine, but if anyone tries anything I'll have no quarrels about making dragon rugs myself."

A groan could be heard in the cave and Solen threw back his head and laughed. "I think they got the message luv, let's go."

Rikar gave her a disgruntled look as she entered the well-lit cavern. "Can see who you take after," he groused, and that had her laughing.

A few more feet inside and her laughter stalled at the sight before her. Treasures all around, gold and jewels neatly in chests with artifacts of all types on shelves, tables and pedestals. Then there were the rows of bookcases full of leather bound books and scrolls. The inside of the cavern was vast, looking up she couldn't even see the ceiling, just bright light. Where the bright light came from she had no idea.

"I think we have mesmerized the beauty."

She had been staring around her in such awe that she hadn't noticed when one of the brothers had come up behind her. She jumped, her arm coming up defensively. Draken raised an eyebrow at her and she gave an abashed look. "Reflexes." She shrugged.

Draken smiled down at her. "No need to be on the defense here, I promise you we come in peace."

Solen snorted. "More like you come on too strong," He shoved at Draken. "Let the lass do some exploring, she has dealt with enough egos in her lifetime."

Calista couldn't stop the giggle that escaped when Draken cuffed Solen upside the head. They reminded her of some of the Greek humans she spied on when Ares wasn't looking. She had always been jealous of them.

Solen stopped and looked at her in surprise, then grinned. "I knew you had a giggle inside you."

She shrugged, walking deeper inside the cavern, looking at all the bountiful treasures around them. Stopping as something just occurred to her, she turned and grinned at Rikar and Draken, who were watching her with interest. "Isn't this a bit ironic?"

They both looked at each other before looking back at her and spoke at the same time. "What?"

"You two are dragon brothers, right?"

They nodded.

"In charge of the treasures of Atlantis?"

"Don't forget, also the history," Rikar spoke, nodding towards the mass of bookshelves.

She laughed. "And history."

They nodded.

"And you put them in a cave?"

They nodded.

She stood there waiting for them to get the reference, it was Solen snickering that made the brothers finally realize she had gotten to the point of what she was trying to say.

Rikar chuckled. "If it works, don't knock it."

"That is Rikar's way of saying they couldn't come up with something original." Solen chuckled then ducked as something round and furry was thrown his way. Calista tried to see what it was but when it scurried off into a dark corner, she decided she didn't need to know that bad.

She left the boys to their male bonding or whatever they were calling it, pushing at each other laughing and trying to out best the other. She was enjoying it but she was also curious about Atlantis. Her home.

Scratch hopped off of her shoulder down to a nearby table full of books, scrolls, gems and golden tools of all sorts. He scurried off to check out this new place; rarely did he leave her side in Greece, always there to protect his mistress.

"Seems your little protector feels comfortable enough to leave you unattended," Solen said to her as he watched her moving about. She barely acknowledged his words, though she knew what he was implying, not that she planned to admit that to him.

She picked up one of the leatherbound books and started to read. It was the story of her grandparents, how they had come together. It was a perfect love story. She curled up into a padded velvet chair that was close, forgetting about the world around her as she read how her grandmother wanted nothing to do with her grandfather at first. It took some sneakiness on her grandfather's part and she discovered that Rowena even had a hand in it.

"Your parent's story is in here as well," Solen spoke beside her, startling her. She had been so engrossed in her reading she hadn't noticed him sitting in a chaise lounge not even three feet from her.

"Is it?" Her eyes lit up and he chuckled.

"It is, but if I don't get you back for the huge feast being thrown in your honor, I might not live to show it to you."

"Here it is." Rikar appeared with the book and an eager expression. She laughed as she took it from him.

"You are a Class A royal pain, you know that?" Solen told him with a baleful look.

Rikar shrugged and laughed. "Our poppa is Poseidon and if you believe all he says, he is the King of the Sea, which would make us royalty."

Calista frowned at him. "Poseidon is the King of the Sea."

Rikar shook his head slowly. "Another poor misguided soul."

Calista frowned and looked at his brother who looked as if he was holding in laughter. "I have a feeling I am going to need to watch the two of you."

They both gave faux expressions of hurt, but she wasn't buying it.

Solen rolled his eyes as he gently took the book from Calista and set it on a small pile of books nearby. Scratch leapt down from a shelf along the wall to his favorite perch on her shoulder. "The book will still be there when you want to read it." He held out his arm and she took it with a smile. He smirked at the dragon brothers, who just shrugged and followed them.

The dinner was something unlike Calista had ever attended. They were all seated around a large oval table that seated everyone. There were no arguments, no loud voices and no one looking down on another. Her grandparents were in deep conversation with Stratos.

Rikar and Draken were whispering to each other, grinning as they kept glancing at Stratos and her grandparents.

Her parents were smiling and chatting with Brine, who kept stealing glances Calista's way. Brine wasn't the only one either. Calista kept feeling eyes upon her and when she would look their way, instead of looking away, the person would just smile at her.

"Think we could pull that stick out and he might actually act normal?" Rikar was asking his brother.

"Rikar!" Her mother admonished him. "Leave Stratos be, he is normal."

Cael snorted. "Normal for him."

"Cael!" Her mother attempted to admonish him but Calista could see the smile in her eyes. The love between the two was obvious and beautiful.

Her father put his arm around the back of Malis' chair. "My heart, you can't deny Stratos is a bit stuffy."

"I prefer the terms reasonable and analytic. In a world ruled by emotions, I am the reason." Stratos's calm voice could be heard above all others.

Many around the table chuckled, Calista had a feeling this wasn't the first time this discussion had happened.

"You call it whatever you want," Rikar told him. "I still think you could stand to loosen up a bit."

"Someone needs to be the voice of reason," Stratos told him. "Do you two seriously think you could handle that, even for an hour?"

"They wouldn't even last a minute." Brine laughed while the brothers attempted to look hurt at her words but Calista saw the twinkle in their eyes.

"Calista." She looked up and Malov was standing by her chair.

"Grandmother," she said with great respect, unsure if she should be addressing her in such a way or if she would get reprimanded for being so familiar with her. When Malov smiled at her, she knew she made the right move.

"I have a gift for you."

Calista didn't know what to say, the only gift she had ever gotten growing up was Zeus giving Scratch immortality. She gasped when Malov opened her hands and there looking up at Calista was Blue.

"Blue!" Calista exclaimed and laughed as her old friend jumped onto her hands. Scratch came out of his hiding place in her hair to say hi to his friend as well. She looked up at Malov. "How?"

"I am the Goddess of Life and Death, I decreed it wasn't her time." Malov held her head high but her smile was nothing but kind.

Calista frowned. "But she was killed in Greece, isn't that Hades' realm?"

Malov smiled and shrugged one shoulder. "What Hades doesn't know won't hurt him."

"It could also fill the ocean," Cael said as he lifted his goblet to take a drink. Calista smiled as she watched Scratch and Blue nuzzle each other in greeting.

Calista looked around the room at all the gods and goddesses who were laughing and joking with one another. They looked at her as part of the family and smiled with acceptance. Solen was sitting between her and the dragon brothers, he had almost fallen into her lap dashing for the seat before Draken, earning him a disapproving look from her grandmother.

Rowena was there, sitting on the other side of Malov with Atmos on her left. So many different personalities in the same room, but the air was one of comradery and pleasantries. The table was overflowing with various types of meats, fruits, grains, and deserts that the dragon brothers were already piling onto their plates.

Her mother leaned over to her. "A dinar for your thoughts, my daughter?"

Calista smiled at her, "I'm happy to finally be home."

Her mother hugged her, "Me too, Cali, me too."

CHAPTER 7

Never had Calista known such peace and acceptance as she had here in Atlantis with her family, her real family. She watched Scratch and Blue playing. At first, she had been concerned about their safety but her mother assured her she had nothing to fear.

They had been walking together after the dinner, just the two of them when Scratch and Blue had jumped from her shoulder to frolic on the grounds. She went to stop them but her mother stopped her.

"Let them have their fun, Cali."

Calista turned back to her mom. "I don't want any harm to come to them."

"No one will harm them here, I promise," her mother assured her.

"And if they did I would make sure they regretted it."

Calista turned to see a redheaded beauty smiling at them, chipmunks in her hair and other creatures at her feet. Not something you would expect to see at the bottom of the ocean.

"Lison." Malis smiled. "Calista, meet our Goddess of Nature and Beauty. Lison, meet my daughter, Calista."

"I heard our darling Calista finally returned home." Lison smiled at her. "I'm happy to see that you have attuned yourself to our eight-legged friends, they get such a bad rap but yet are one of the most beneficial creatures to grace our world."

That was last night and now Calista was seated on one of the many ornate benches around Atlantis. She smiled remembering how Lison had petted the spiders and spoke fondly of them, no one in Atlantis seemed upset by their presence. She was truly glad that Solen had convinced her to come.

"Drachma for your thoughts?"

Speak of the devil, there was the subject of her thoughts, grinning down at her.

"Is Drachma even the currency here in Atlantis?"

Solen just shrugged and handed her the flower he had been hiding behind his back, "How about a beautiful blossom for your thoughts?"

She laughed and took the flower. "My thoughts aren't that interesting," she assured him.

He sat next to her. "I wouldn't sell yourself short there, goddess."

Calista just shrugged. "Same thoughts I've had since you brought me here."

"And that is?" He watched her closely with that intense look of his.

"How different this place is from Greece. Everywhere I look I see the differences." Calista looked over to where

Atmos and Brine were talking with a few of their acolytes. "You wouldn't see the gods of Greece talking with their worshipers like that, humans to them are more like playthings."

"In many ways it is different, but like in all cultures, there are some similarities." Solen shrugged. "You just have to decide if those similarities are something you can live with."

She wasn't sure what he was talking about but there was something in his voice that tugged at her feelings. "What about your culture?"

He looked shocked at the question. "My culture? Why would you ask about that?"

"Well, you know all about mine." She smelled the flower. "I would like to know about the guy who came into the hornet's nest to bring home someone he didn't even know."

A strange look came over Solen's face but it disappeared so quickly, Calista wondered if she imagined it.

Solen shrugged, his gaze darting all around them. "There isn't much to tell, I am a hunter who got hired to bring home the princess."

Before Calista could inquire any further, a ball came from nowhere and hit Solen on the back of his head.

"Hey loverboy, what ya doing?" Rikar shouted as he plopped down on the bench beside Solen while Draken sat down on the other side of Calista, placing his arm along the back.

"Be careful, brother, you could have hurt this beautiful lady." Draken winked at Calista, who laughed. She had come to enjoy the brothers during her short time in Atlantis.

Calista turned and saw Solen staring at her with a weird grin on his face. "What?"

"It's nice to see you smile."

"You've only known me for a short while." Calista frowned at him, sure she would remember seeing him before.

"What our compliment-inept friend here is trying to say is that you are beautiful when you smile." Draken smiled down at her.

She couldn't stop the laughter that overflowed. Draken was quite the charmer.

"Not just when she smiles, brother." Rikar winked at her before Solen shoved him to the ground. She moved to help but Draken put his hand on her shoulder and smiled.

"Let's let them settle this between themselves while you sit here and tell me more about you." He grinned at her. Charmer was probably too tame of a word for this dragon.

She looked down where Solen and Rikar were wrestling on the ground when she caught a movement out of the corner of her eye. Rowena watched from the shadows. She smiled at Draken. "How about you help them settle the matter while I go check on something?"

She laughed at the disappointed look on his face but could see him entering the fray as she walked towards Rowena who watched her approach.

"Are you enjoying yourself, Calista?" Rowena asked, her lips curling into a smile.

"Yes, I am," Calista said then frowned at her. "But I get the feeling that isn't the reason you're here."

"As I said, smart like your mother." Rowena smiled at Calista then motioned for her to follow her. "Let's go for a walk while the boys are playing."

With a nod Calista followed Rowena as she moved along the pathway along the outskirts of Atlantis. Rowena's feet barely touched the ground, it was as if she were walking on air. Calista looked around them as they walked. The beauty of Atlantis drew her in and she had even seen the exalted Olympus. Olympus was more sterile in appearance, while beneath the surface lay chaos, greed, and corruption. Atlantis was more lively and all she had felt since coming was acceptance and love.

If she were honest with herself, deep down she worried that this was all a ruse and would soon fall around her in flames.

"Atlantis wasn't always beneath the water," Rowena spoke softly as they walked. "Before the curse, we walked in the sun."

"The curse Ares brought upon you," Calista said, to which Rowena nodded.

"Yes."

Calista ran her hand down the rough surface of the nearest tree with its colorful flowers, she had a feeling there was something of importance with Rowena's request for them to walk together. She learned long ago that silence would bring more answers than questions. So she waited and walked.

"That curse has ruled our lives for so long now we have almost forgotten what the world above feels like." Rowena turned to look at Calista. "But that curse has also caused hard feelings with many."

Calista frowned. "That's to be expected, everyone here lost a lot with that curse."

"And they stand to lose a lot more."

"What do you mean?" Calista had just found her home and family, she wasn't ready to lose it all. Not now, not ever.

Rowena glided over to where you could see the boundary of Atlantis, the wall of water that surrounded the whole city. With just one touch of her fingers, the wall came alive with images, causing Calista to gasp in wonder and Rowena laugh.

"I am the Goddess of Magic and Whimsy, you didn't think my magic was tied to just my fountain?"

Calista looked chagrined but Rowena only laughed.

"My magic is as endless as Ixion's punishment."

Calista raised a brow and wrinkled her nose. "Couldn't you think of a better example than one of the many punishments Zeus likes to dole out?"

"Something that is almost as unending as Hera's

jealousies." Rowena laughed and Calista couldn't stop her own laughter.

"Can't argue with facts." Calista chuckled.

Rowena gave a solemn nod that silenced Calista's chuckles, Rowena's expression had become as solemn as her voice. "Sadly, that is the case."

With her words, the water swirled and images of a great battle appeared all around them. Calista gasped when she saw Ares in full battle armor. Across the battlefield, a figure stood in majestic armor with blond hair flowing from the helmet she wore, clutching a silver sword etched with symbols Calista had seen in the caves with the brothers and Solen.

"Your mother," Rowena stated.

Calista had already figured that out, she had felt a connection with the formidable figure that stood there with the impressive army behind her. She was sure she could see her father as well, his armor not as impressive as her mother's, some dings and not as shiny. Her mouth dropped a bit when she realized what she was seeing. It was Atlanteans and Greeks going into battle with each other.

"Is this the past you are showing me?" Calista knew it wasn't, but she had hoped. A hope that was dashed with a shake of Rowena'shead.

"I only wish, the battle between Atlantis and Greece never came to fruition," Rowena sighed. "This battle is the future, very near future."

"Aren't you going to do anything about it?"

"I have tried, but they won't listen to me," Rowena spoke softly as the images started to move towards one another, their weapons raised as lightning flashed across the sky and the sounds of waves crashing could be heard. "We created a home here beneath the waters in the years you were taken from us. I had thought the vengeance and anger had waned.

"I was foolish," Rowena turned towards Calista. "Time did nothing to heal those wounds, the wounds were ..." She paused, taking a deep breath and corrected herself. "Are too deep. The Greeks not only took you away from us, they also imprisoned us beneath the water with no way to see the sun again."

"But now that I'm back, the curse is broken."

Rowena nodded.

"Why start a war now?"

"Because we are now free to do so."

"I thought Atlantis was more benign than the barbaric Greeks?" Calista frowned, this was something she would expect of the Greek gods. Was she once again being foolish in thinking that she had found peace?

"My dear, Atlanteans ... Greeks ... we are still gods and we have more faults than the humans that worship us." Rowena's images changed with her words, showing different gods and goddesses from different Pantheons, not only Greek and Atlantis.

"But unlike humans, we have powers."

"Which makes our faults even worse." Rowena

nodded to the images where it showed Arachne, the one who Calista had always believed to be her mother. "Cursed by Athena for her pride." Then the water showed the stars where the constellation of Ursa Major shone. "The nymph Callisto, cursed because she caught Zeus's eye."

"But what do these have to do with the Atlantean gods?"

"The Pantheon doesn't matter, Calista. Power is decadent and can taint even the purest of heart or intention."

"You are saying even the Atlanteans are no different than the Greeks?"

The images all shifted until there were but only two, Ares standing there in his dented and bloodied armor alongside Malis with her shiny, pristine armor. The two deities of war. Different sides of the same coin.

"Of course we are different, my child. But that doesn't mean we don't have our faults." The images faded. "Our people have been angry and wanting to strike out for so long. And now they are able to."

"What about Stratos? Can't he stop this?"

"The Greeks are in the wrong, so in his eyes our retribution is due to us."

"You have to do something to stop this, it won't solve anything. It won't bring back those years."

Rowena looked at her. "Only you can do that."

Calista stared at her then turned around and walked away. She wasn't sure how but she was going to stop this war before it destroyed all that had become dear to her.

CHAPTER 8

Her mother's temple was so different from Ares', which happened to be full of statues and paintings of the god himself. Her mother's temple was full of color and life. Flowers, paintings, and maps of lands from all over filled the walls. The air was more welcome than any of Ares' temples where blood and bones were commonplace. She walked down the lit corridor from the entryway looking for her mother.

"Why am I the only one who can stop a war?" she grumbled to herself as she looked through the empty rooms for her mother. She wasn't sure how she was going to stop this war but was sure the answer had something to do with her mother. Her mother was the Goddess of War after all, if she could convince her mother this was insane then maybe her mother would be able to convince the others. After all, her mother knew them better than she.

The sound of voices ahead had her turning the corner and entering a room full of Atlanteans, both gods and goddesses, many she hadn't had a chance to meet yet. What she saw had her stomach sinking and her faith in being able to stop this war waning. Her mother was standing before a map of Greece, one that showed all the temples of the Greek gods and goddesses.

Her mother wasn't in full war armor, but she wore a silver headpiece with gold etchings all around. She looked fierce and commanding as she spoke of strategic offense and the best places to target their attacks.

There was one dark-haired male that was standing off to the side watching with an intensity that made her uncomfortable. She hadn't met him yet but now wasn't the time to meet new friends or family, depending on which one he was.

"Mother." Calista stepped further into the room. "What's going on?"

Calista couldn't stop the flashbacks that filled her thoughts as she entered that room, the times she had entered the war room of Ares only to become the target of his ire. His generals would sneer as he would belittle her or toss her across the room for daring to interrupt him and his generals. Rowena told her she was the only one who could stop the war. She hoped she was right and she wasn't about to get a feeling of deja vu.

Malis stopped and held up her hand to silence her general who was speaking. "Daughter, what are you doing here? You should be with the dragons and Solen, learning about Atlantis."

Her mother didn't sound angry which gave Calista a bit more bravado. "While my mother plans a war between pantheons?"

"How could you not understand us wanting to get back at the Greeks for what they did to us?" Salis asked her. The God of Agriculture and Inspiration was dressed in war attire decorated with wheat symbols and looking fierce.

She looked at her uncle. "Because I've found my family and to me, everyone here is more important than revenge. War brings nothing but heartache." She looked back at her mother. "It was Ares who cursed us all, not the other gods and goddesses."

"You really think the other gods and goddesses will just stand idly by and let us take out one of their own?" Atmos asked her from his position next to her mother at the war table.

"Why attack anyone?" Calista looked around the room. "The curse is broken, there is no reason for a conflict of any kind."

"Aren't you the one who swore vengeance against Strife for killing your little blue friend?" The dark god who stood in the shadows asked her. "Or even Apollo?"

Calista barely contained the urge to slap him, bringing up that instance was out of line as far as she was concerned. It also brought up some explosive emotions within her, that took her many moments to push down.

"I won't deny that I've imagined many moments of retribution against those that have wronged me, but being here and seeing all the love and acceptance, and feeling it with all of you here." She looked at everyone except for the one dark god still standing in the shadows.

"I have learned there is more to life than revenge and war. I don't want to spend another thought on those who have wronged me, they have taken enough away from me. From all of us." She looked at her mother praying that her mother would understand.

Malis smiled at her and moved closer, raising her hand to rest on Calista's shoulder. "My daughter may be young, but she speaks with the knowledge of one who has lived many years."

Calista stared at her mother unsure of what to say, she was so unused to compliments of any type that it took her several moments to realize her mother was talking about her. She gave a tentative smile, moving her hand to place it on top of her mother's. "Thank you, Mother."

"So, am I to take it that because your daughter doesn't have the stomach for war, we're going to cancel our only chance to take the Greeks by surprise?" the dark god in the shadows asked Malis, his voice dripping of disdain.

"Brax." Her mother frowned at him. "Calista's right, we've no reason to start a war. The curse is broken and I have my daughter back."

"So, we're to forget all the years we have been prisoners beneath the waves?" Brax asked in his deep disapproving tone. "Just forget everything they have done?"

"Brax has a point." This god that spoke was shorter in stature than the others and looked a bit out of place with all the other gods and goddesses. He wasn't in any type of armor, he stood there in breeches and a cotton shirt that Calista had seen many of the Greek mortal boys running around in.

"We forget nothing." Cael stood by his wife and daughter, winking at Calista. "Nor will we forgive, but we also won't spend another minute of our time on people who aren't worth it. We are free and we have our family home, now is the time to move forward and not backward."

"So, should I take it that I should no longer keep an eye on them then?" Brax spoke, his voice was becoming like fingernails on a chalkboard to Calista.

"Of course not." Malis shook her head. "Just because we aren't attacking them doesn't mean we're going to trust them, we'll continue to watch them carefully. We won't be surprised by them again. You and Rowena will keep vigilant with them, but if they do nothing against us then we'll leave them be."

Atmos snorted. "They're Greeks, just leave them alone and they will take themselves out with their combative nature."

"Atmos," Malis gave a gentle chiding, but Calista saw the smile on her face. "Now, let's put all this war talk away. We'll fortify our defenses but we won't attack."

Calista gave her mom a grateful smile.

"You never wanted this war did you?" Brax spoke right behind Malis as she watched her daughter and husband smiling with the other Atlanteans.

"I don't know what you mean, Braxton," Malis spoke in her gentle way, calling the God of Duality by his full name.

"You're playing a dangerous game, Malis. You can't hide your head in the sand forever, sooner or later you'll have to come up for air."

Malis turned to him and gave a small smile. "I think seeing the beginning and ending of so much has turned you cynical Braxton, I miss the old Brax who knew how to smile and enjoy life."

A dark brow raised at her words. "Seeing the beginning and ending of all things is why I know we need this war, we need to have the advantage, Malis."

Malis turned once again to watch her daughter, the daughter she had feared never being able to hold again. "You see the beginnings and endings of everything, but even you've admitted the endings are subject to change."

"You really want to take that chance?"

Malis turned and looked directly into his eyes. "Unless you want to tell me exactly why we need this war." She waved her hand dismissively. "I don't want to hear about your rules, what I really want to know is what you had to do to return my daughter to me. What deal did you make?"

"Are you regretting the deal now?"

"Of course not, I would have done anything to get my daughter back." Malis frowned at him, hating him for his detached attitude.

"I warned you all that the deal could come at a heavy price, a war with Greece. No one argued it then."

"Because we believed Greece would attack us and we would be defending our loved ones and home, not that we would be the aggressors."

Brax turned his head slightly, his black eyes looking into hers. "I never promised that, I only promised the return of your daughter and a war."

"I won't start a war without due cause. Our pantheon is just starting to heal, a war could tear it more apart than it already is. Especially an unprovoked one."

"Your daughter isn't good enough reason to?"

"The Greeks haven't made a move against us for her, unless you know something we don't."

Brax moved from the wall he had been casually leaning against and let his gaze travel slowly over the room. "I always know something that you don't, Malis, you know that. You also know I can't tell you everything, it could change something that shouldn't be changed."

"You can't expect us to go into a battle blind, with no information."

Brax snorted as he motioned towards the maps labeled with positions and the documents littering the war table with the intel they had gathered on the Greeks during their exile.

"You know what I mean, to rally troops to a war you need a cause. A just one, or else we're no better than those we attack."

Brax gave a shrug. "Who knows, maybe I'm wrong and we won't need this war." He looked at her. "Maybe we can continue to live down beneath the waves with our heads in the sand and no one will even notice us." With those words, he turned and walked away.

"Brax!" Malis called after him but he still kept walking. She sighed. If not for him they would never have gotten her daughter back nor would they have broken this curse. She owed him so much, but to start a war with little to no information simply isn't done, he had to understand that. She just wished she knew why a war with the Greek gods was so important to him.

When Brax informed them he had a way to bring Calista home and break the curse, she had been so happy, even when he said it would bring war with the Greeks. Something the whole Atlantean pantheon was not only ready for but they thought they truly wanted. A chance for retribution.

She had assumed it would be from them being the attackers, not the other way around. Her daughter thankfully gave her the perfect out. Her daughter, who had more reasons than any of them to want retribution, was ready to turn the other cheek. She gave a soft sigh and moved into the room to be with her husband and daughter. She would worry about Brax's motives much later.

CHAPTER 9

It had been weeks since Calista stopped the war between the Greeks and Atlanteans, she had spent her days exploring Atlantis and learning all she could from the dragon brothers. Draken and Rikar were knowledgeable. When they weren't trying to be charming or poking at Solen, they had become her scholars of Atlantean history. She had her own desk in the caves where she learned from them. Books, parchment, and quills covered the top of her desk with little artifacts she had taken to and placed in certain spots.

Her favorite was a wooden bridge with stones that held the Atlantean alphabet, the letters were etched onto stone looking wooden blocks that could only be placed back into their place in a certain order. "This is what every Atlantean child learns on." Rikar told her.

Atlantis was a world of wonders, not only its history, but everything. It wasn't only gods and goddesses who lived here but many others. Nymphs, shifters and so many other creatures all lived together in harmony. Well, for the most part. Just like anywhere, you had some tensions and arguments.

She was the granddaughter of the rulers of Atlantis, everywhere she went others showed her respect she never thought would ever be shown to her. She spent most of her life hiding her emotions for fear they would be used against her, she had to be hard and tough to survive. All she had ever known was pain and anger, now she had friends and family that cared about her and not just for what use she could be to them.

As Calista stood there lost in thought, a movement caught her eye, a willowy redhead who was walking the border of Atlantis. What used to be their prison walls was now protecting them from the ocean around them all thanks to Rowena. The wall that kept them ensconced within the borders of Atlantis started to deteriorate shortly after Calista arrived. She had broken the curse that kept them here, which meant the barrier around them all. She had been walking along the border with Scratch who was right now watching the redhead, something she had taken to doing after her teachings and trainings with the brothers and Solen.

Letting her mind go back to wandering, she thought about the emergency council that had been called to decide if they wanted to attempt to go back to the surface where they had come from.

"We should take back what's rightfully ours," Vesper, the God of Chaos stated. He had a wild look in his dark eyes, his white hair flying around his head in permanent chaos.

"What's rightfully ours is what we see around us," his sister Vapor said calmly, seated on his right. Her eyes as white as her brother's hair while her hair, black, long and flat as it settled around her shoulders. A complete contrast to her brother. Her expression was very serene and calm, befitting her title, Goddess of Calm and Tranquility. Whenever her brother attempted to start chaos, she would appear and ruin his fun. He grumbled many times that he would have more fun in Greece.

"Vapor is right," Salis spoke up. "That's no longer our world up there, we've made a home down here beneath the waves and many of our inhabitants are from the waters around us who ended up trapped here, unable to return home. Do we leave them just to go back to a world that doesn't even believe in us anymore?"

There were many nods at his words and murmurs of agreement around the table and room. Brax, the dark one Calista remembered from her mother's war room, stared at her, making her uncomfortable. So when he moved forward into the room she tensed up, sure she wouldn't like whatever it was he was about to say.

"Let's hear what our newest member of the family has to say about this." He stared at her waiting for her answer. She wondered if she would get in trouble for slapping him.

"What do you think, granddaughter?" Tylaos asked her and she was speechless for a moment. Her grandmother, mother, and father have spoken to her many times since she arrived, but she hadn't had much time with her grandfather. He was an imposing figure although he had shown her nothing but kindness each encounter.

She swallowed hard but spoke up. "I've lived on the land all my life in the sun and was nothing but miserable. Down here under the water with everyone who is here, I've never been happier. Everyone has made a home down here and I don't see why anyone needs to uproot themselves to go back to a world where you would have to reintroduce yourself." Calista noticed a strange look in Brax's eye but she ignored him. "Besides, up on the surface you will have many enemies whose only goal will be to usurp you again. Down here, you should already know who is your friend and enemy." The last was said while staring at Brax, who smiled at her and nodded as if her words pleased him.

"But the barrier is disappearing, the waters will destroy our homes and possessions if we don't do something," Lison spoke up.

"I don't think so," Rowena rose from her seat next to Malov. "I believe that I can use my magic to turn the barrier into a veil that we can move freely between."

Tylaos looked at her. "You think you can do such a thing, Rowena?" She nodded confidently. "Then let it be done, we will stay here and rule our pantheon under the waves."

So, now, everyone can move freely through the veil

from Atlantis to the ocean floor. Mostly it was the creatures that came from the waters in the first place ,such as the redhead beauty Calista was watching and trying to figure out who or what she was. When the redhead walked through the veil into the watery depths, her legs started to shine as scales popped out and joined her legs as one tail with very silky fins.

"A siren." Calista smiled as the siren swam away. It was wonderful watching all the creatures who had come to call Atlantis home.

"Shayna," a voice spoke from behind her. Turning around, she saw a dark-haired female staring down at her. "A sister of mine." When Calista still looked confused she nodded towards the water where the siren had disappeared.

"You're a siren?"

The female raised a brow and her voice was sarcastic. "Can't get anything past you."

This had Calista taken aback, that manner was something commonplace in Greece but not here in Atlantis. "Excuse me?"

The siren snorted. "My name is Sylla and yes I am a siren, just like my sister Shayna you saw. I had thought with your parentage you would have more brains than most down here. I guess living amongst the Greeks had to have some damage on you."

Seems even Atlantis has their own share of Discords and Strifes.

"Shayna caught the dragon brothers' eyes, for a short time. If she couldn't keep their interest for more than a date, I highly doubt you will," Sylla spoke with a smile on her face but her words were full of malice.

"I'm afraid I don't understand what you are trying to say." Surely Sylla wasn't implying that she was after the brothers?

"I'm pretty sure you do." Sylla stared at her and that was when Calista saw that the smile Sylla gave her was full of venom just as the eyes that looked at her. Was this jealousy?

"If you're jealous of Draken and Rikar I can assure you that I've no romantic interest in them, they've just been teaching me about Atlantis and its history," Calista tried to assure her.

"Just make sure that's all they teach you, I wouldn't want you to get hurt thinking their affection might actually mean more than the dalliance it truly is." Sylla gave another venomous smile then turned smartly around and stalked away. She didn't go to the water like her sister but rather back to the center of Atlantis where most of the inhabitants lived.

She sighed, she knew she couldn't expect everyone here to be friendly and sweet. That would truly be too much to ask for. Although if she was honest with herself, she had truly hoped that was going to be the case.

She wasn't sure if she felt sorry for Sylla or annoyed. After all, she knew the brothers were incorrigible flirts who didn't seem to want to settle for one love. Rather they seemed to want to experience an enjoyable time with all the pretty ladies. Was Sylla an ex or just a hopeful?

She walked towards the veil and stared into the depths as a Seelie swam by and smiled at her. She saw some water nymphs who were waving at her and waving for her to join them. She laughed but shook her head.

"Come on, princess, can't let down your people."

Rikar lifted Calista in his arms and threw them both through the veil into the water around them. She turned to slap him and found herself looking into the blue eyes of a water dragon who grinned at her. She slapped him then turned to go back through the veil but another water dragon was grinning down at her. Bad enough that they were taller than her in human form, but boy, in dragon form they were massive!

She sent an energy wave at Draken knocking him back. Laughing, Calista attempted to swim away but the water around her started to swirl quickly around and she found herself in a funnel of water.

Play nice, princess, or we will have to put you in a timeout.

Play nice? She was brought up with Discord and Strife, she was never taught how to play nice. With a grin, she turned the water funnel on them so that they were the ones spinning around, then turned and swam away from them but some Kelpies swimming by stopped her. Gorgeous horse creatures she so longed to ride.

We can take you riding on one, princess.

She rolled her eyes at Draken who had gotten out of the water funnel way too easily and had already caught up to her, along with his brother. She was about to respond to them when a hand snaked into the water and pulled her back through the veil.

There stood Solen, who frowned at the brothers. The brothers sauntered back through the veil grinning at Solen, unabashed at their playing. "The princess looked like she could do with some fun, mate." Rikar grinned at him.

"Besides, I don't see your ownership on the princess anywhere." Draken shrugged at him.

"Her pet was worried about her, he came to get me right after you pulled her through the veil," Solen told them, his brow furrowed at them still.

Sure enough Scratch was already climbing up to sit on her shoulder, his leg reaching out to scratch at her neck as if to reassure himself that his mistress was indeed okay. She laughed and nuzzled her little friend. "I'm all right baby, I promise."

"See, no harm is done." Draken grinned and put his arm around her.

She shrugged off his arm, laughing. "With the veil open now, I'm surprised you two aren't off romancing all the pretty ladies that have had to live their lives without your flattery and gestures."

It was Rikar who responded this time. "But there is no one that could compete with you, princess."

She rolled her eyes at them and walked away laughing. "I'm sure that is a big exaggeration and how many times do I have to keep telling you guys, I'm not a princess."

"About a few more thousand might do it," She could hear the grin in Rikar's voice. Those brothers were something else but she did enjoy their company. She looked back and saw Solen staring intently after her. She enjoyed him as well but felt as if he was holding something back from her.

She had been so happy since coming to Atlantis, she never thought it possible and she worried something would ruin it. After all, isn't that what usually happens?

CHAPTER 10

"Go long!"

Calista was going through the scrolls in the caves while the brothers were goofing around with a shell they had found on the ocean floor, Scratch watching them from a shelf above Calista with interest. Blue, who had become comfortable here in Atlantis, was sitting with Scratch. While Scratch was her permanent companion Blue enjoyed her freedom as she explored Atlantis. She laughed as Solen quickly moved a vase out of Rikar's way as he toppled over a chaise lounge. She wasn't sure how the caves weren't full of broken ceramics. Of course, Rowena would probably skin them alive if that happened.

The brothers seemed to be scared of Rowena, or at least they tried their hardest not to aggravate her. Unlike Calista, who reached up just as the sea shell landed in her hand. She turned to look at the smiling trio.

"Is this how you study?"

Draken smirked at her. "We don't need to study princess, we're here to school you."

"Is this how you teach?" She leaned back against the seat, looking up at them.

"Come on, princess, all work and no fun makes us dull dragons." Rikar winked at her.

"You don't want to be responsible for making the favorite dragon brothers stagnant." Draken gave her a flirtatious look that she ignored.

She had been looking through old prophecies and the history of the royal family of Atlantis, her family. It started with the book of her parents' story, a story that made her laugh, smile and cry.

At first, she had been amazed that she was able to read the scriptures and stories so easily. Well, that was till Rikar burst her bubble.

"I can read Atlantean!" She had said proudly, grinning at all three of them.

Rikar raised a brow. "All Atlanteans can read Atlantean."

"Yeah, but I wasn't born here."

Rikar leaned back in his chair and grinned at her. "All Atlanteans can read Atlantean."

Calista gave an exasperated sigh. "BUT, I wasn't born here," she said again, giving him a hard stare, daring him to say that again.

Rikar smirked and opened his mouth, she conjured an energy ball in her hand ready to knock his ass off that chair.

Solen moved quickly between the two. "What Rikar is so eloquently trying to say in his irritating manner is that even if you didn't grow up in Atlantis you could still read Atlantean. Atlanteans are born with the ability to read Atlantean. Outsiders cannot."

Rikar rolled his eyes. "Solen, you're becoming one hell of a stick in the coral."

"Think he has caught the bug, my brother." Draken leaned against his brother's chair, looking between Solen and Calista.

Rikar shrugged. "No ring, no sign." Then he rose and grinned at Calista. "And you, princess, were most assuredly born here, you may have been taken away shortly after your birth but you were born here." With that Rikar and Draken had left Calista with Solen.

Since that day Calista had spent as much time as she could in the caves with the scrolls and tablets, enjoying reading and learning about the history of her family. There were scrolls of history, innovations, astrology and prophecies. The shelves were full of complete sets that kept her interest as she read through as many as she could, although there was one set that wasn't as complete as the others. There was a set of prophecies that spoke of gods from the stars as well as some false gods.

"Arrgh!" she yelled, startling Scratch and Blue, who were napping on a shelf above her desk as well as startling the three guys who were playing catch.

Solen leaped over a bench and was at her side. "What's wrong, Spider?"

She gave a frustrated grunt and pointed to an empty slot in the shelves. "Where is it?"

Solen frowned. "Where is what?"

"There is a missing scroll that should be there." Calista glared at the offending empty spot.

Draken chuckled. "Glaring won't make the scroll appear with its tail between its legs, princess."

"I don't know, brother, that look could make me come running." Rikar winked at her and she just rolled her eyes.

"You two are the keepers of the archives and treasures of Atlantis." Calista placed her hands on her hips and stared at them.

Draken chuckled. "You wanted the look brother, all yours." He laughed and plopped down on a padded chaise lounge, his arm draped across the back.

Rikar moved closer to Calista with a grin. "That is fine, brother, you can stay there while I work on turning that frown into a smile."

"Wait a minute," Draken protested and stood up quickly. "I didn't say that."

"Too late." His brother grinned.

Solen moved so that he was between Rikar and Calista who was about to shimmer the brothers right into the ocean, except she needed answers.

"Enough!" She spoke loudly, causing the whole room to still. The brothers looked at her from their frozen positions. Looking at Solen, she saw he was just as still, that was when she realized she was the reason that they were frozen in place. She had grown up as a goddess with hardly any powers, treated differently and with contempt by her family and peers. Since coming home to Atlantis things were changing for her, she was starting to come into her powers and it was a good feeling.

The sound of a throat clearing made her realize that they were still frozen. Releasing them, she gave a chagrined smile. "Sorry about that."

Solen shrugged and grinned at her. "No apology necessary Spider, we were annoying you."

"Speak for yourself," Draken muttered. "I didn't even get a chance."

Before it turned into another wrestling match, Calista pointed to the empty spot. "Where is the scroll that was there?"

Rikar looked at the slot and frowned. "It was stolen."

"By whom?"

"The traitor." Draken wore the same aggravated look and his words had Calista pressing her lips together.

The traitor. She knew nothing about this person except their temple was in a dilapidated state that no one entered, this person was the one who delivered her to Ares as an infant and that no one here in Atlantis spoke this person's name.

"Does anyone know what was on the scroll?"

Draken and Rikar both shook their heads. "No, the night he disappeared with you, that scroll was also found missing along with many others," Draken spoke and then nodded to the table where there were many other scrolls in slotted shelves. Some of the holes were full but you could see spaces where some were missing as well. Calista grumbled, she hated getting half information.

Calista entered her grandparents' temple with the brothers and Solen. Stopping inside the door, she stared at the three people that were talking to her grandparents and parents. She had never seen them before. They didn't look like any of the Atlanteans she had met, but then again since the veil had dropped, Atlantis had seen an influx of outside visitors.

There were three of them, all with silver hair and pale skin. The one who seemed to be the leader of the group had short silver hair, while the two behind him had long hair. They wore long white robes that covered the white breeches they wore and on their feet were white sandals. If they stood against the pristine white marble of her grandparent's temple, they would simply blend in. The leader turned to look at her with silver eyes, it was as if there were no color whatsoever on these people.

Were they gods?

"Calista!" Her mother smiled at her, genuinely pleased to see her, and motioned for her to join them. Calista turned to the boys standing behind her only to see the dragon brothers looking curious as well. Solen's demeanor had changed, he went from relaxed and joking to standing upright and alert. She frowned at that.

"Solen, be at ease, there is no one here that means us harm." The modulated voice had her turning back to look at the visitors who were all staring at her now, even as the leader addressed Solen. She turned back to Solen to notice he wasn't as stiff but she could tell he was still alert and not looking her way at all. "We've just come to make sure everything went as planned and we see that it has. You've done us a great service."

Solen nodded but didn't ease his posture.

Calista moved closer to her mother, making sure to keep a wide berth between her and the silver ones.

"Fear not child, we mean you no harm." The leader spoke to her kindly, but still in that modulated tone. Calista was sure she had never been around anyone so perfect, their appearance and their words. Even Janus, who tried to be the most controlled Greek god, couldn't pull it off.

Malis put her arm around Calista. "These are the Ancients, daughter, they were the ones who helped us bring you home. They are gods and goddesses who travel the stars. They helped break the curse that kept us prisoners beneath the waves."

Calista nodded to them in respect, but yet felt as if something wasn't right.

The leader approached her. "My name is Lux and my associates here are Loom and Lore." Each nodded their head respectively when their name was spoken. Which was a good thing, because while you could tell one was male and one was female, their names were pretty bland and nothing that could tell you which was which. "You have already met our hunter, Solen."

Calista jerked and looked at Solen, who was still staring straight ahead and not at her. When she first met Solen he had called himself that, but she never truly understood it. "Hunter?"

"Yes, he is our best hunter. Which is why we sent him to find you." Lux nodded to her then looked at Tylaos. "There is still the subject of payment to be discussed."

Tylaos laughed. "Yes, yes, but first let us celebrate our victory, Lux."

Loom and Lore frowned but Lux held up his hand as if to silence them. "I forgot you Atlanteans love your celebrations."

Malov wrapped her arm around Tylaos's waist and smiled at them. "For many years we had nothing to celebrate, now thanks to you Ancients, we do and we would like to honor you for that."

"The payment is the honor." Lore spoke for the first time, his tone as monotonous as Lux but Calista felt a hint of irritation there as well.

Malis laughed and hugged her daughter. "But you've been instrumental in bringing home the heart of our family, we must celebrate."

Lux nodded. "Very well, we'll partake in your

celebration and then discuss payment afterward." He turned to look at Lore and Loom. "Until the celebration, we'll retire to our vessel." Lux turned back around and gave a small bow to Calista. "We'll be seeing you again." With that, they turned and left, as soon as they departed Solen's demeanor relaxed and he gave Calista one of his signature grins.

CHAPTER 11

"Why didn't you tell me about being a Hunter?"

Calista and Solen were walking around Atlantis heading to the royal temple where the celebration of the Ancients was being held.

Solen looked everywhere except at her. "I told you I was a Hunter when we first met."

Calista stopped and turned to him, her brow furrowed. "Yes, you did, but you never truly told me what it meant."

Solen looked at her. "A Hunter hunts and that is what I did."

"So I was just a job?" Calista's brow furrowed at him.

Solen shook his head, "No, you weren't just a job, Spider. Yes, I was sent to search you out, to bring you home by the Ancients who were employed by your family. I found you many years before I showed myself to you."

She opened her mouth to say something before shutting it and looking around, her tongue darting out to moisten her lips. Finally, after a few moments she turned her head to look back at Solen, who was watching her with an expression that she had never seen on his face before. "I never saw you before that day on the cliffs."

"No," he admitted. "I watched from afar until the time was right to approach you."

She looked down not sure how to feel, her fingers lacing together in front of her. Solen lifted her chin with one finger as he looked at her. "I saw a strong woman who never let the pettiness of those around her keep her down, always came back up with her head held high when they would knock her down. Each time you showed how you had more class and greatness than all of them combined."

This conversation was starting to make her feel uncomfortable, as she started chewing on her bottom lip. She didn't know how to react to his words, the way he spoke of her was not something she was used to. She would try to figure out that later, right now she was curious about something else. "So, when did you become one of their Hunters?"

"Since the day the Ancients saved my world, and I'm their only Hunter." Solen turned away and started walking towards the temple.

"Your world?" Calista had to run to catch up to him as his words momentarily stunned her. Grabbing his arm to stop him, she asked, "What do you mean your world?"

He had a sad look in his eyes when he looked at her.

"I'm not from around here, little Spider, I was brought here to find you."

Calista frowned at him. "But the way the brothers speak of you, you've been here for a long time." Just as she said that something else clicked in her mind. "If you've been here for so long, how did you leave Atlantis when others couldn't?"

"Because I'm not from around here, the curse only affected those from this world." One of his shoulders lifted as if to say it wasn't important.

"You keep saying worlds, don't you mean pantheons? And that doesn't make any sense. The brothers are Greek, and they were still affected."

Solen sighed. "No, little Spider, I mean worlds." With those softly spoken words, he kept walking towards the royal temple where there were lights and music that could be heard. Calista followed him, still not understanding his words but feeling the sadness in them as well as something else she couldn't put her finger on. Something that didn't sit right with her.

"Hey Brax, look, it's your people! They've the same personality as you … none!"

Calista tried to hold back the grin as Rikar joked around during the celebration. Rowena sent them a look that had Calista pursing her lips and trying to look serious, but the brothers just grinned. She looked around for Solen but couldn't see him. As soon as they entered the temple he had disappeared and the brothers found her.

"Relax, princess, Solen will find you soon enough." Draken grinned down at her.

"Agreed, until then enjoy your time with us." Rikar took her hand and led her out to the floor and twirled her around. She laughed as they danced along with the others, Rikar would bow and twirl her right into his brother's arms. Draken would then bow and lead her around before twirling her back into his brother's arms.

"You guys are going to make me dizzy." She laughed at them.

"Everyone!" They turned and there they saw her grandparents, parents, the Ancients, and Solen standing there. "Let us thank the Ancients for bringing our Calista home to us." The roar of applause was deafening and Calista felt her face warm.

"You would think they could smile for their own party."

Calista looked at Atmos in his colorful robes. "Why don't they smile?"

"The Ancients are gods and goddesses from the stars." Stratos appeared and for once both the dragon brothers straightened up. Not many could elicit that kind of response from the brothers. Calista frowned as his words gave her a sense of déjà vu, Stratos continued speaking, either not noticing her frown or not caring.

"They believe in structure and order. They also excel in it, so much that they have removed emotions that could cloud that structure and order." Stratos looked at them. "They are to be commended, after all they've saved us all."

"How did they save us all?" Calista asked him.

"They found you and brought you home," he told her. "That broke the curse around Atlantis."

"Solen found me and brought me home."

"Solen is one of their hunters," Stratos corrected. "Your grandparents and parents summoned the Ancients, thanks to Brax, to break the curse so they could bring you home. So, the Ancients had Solen bring you home, which broke the curse."

"Brax?" Calista looked over at the god in question, who was staring at the Ancients with an intense expression.

"Yes, he discovered a way to reach out from our prison and contact the Ancients to request their help. The Ancients are ethereal beings from the stars, they are known for being able to create miracles you never thought possible, for a price." Stratos spoke with a nod of his head.

"So, when are we going to find out what their payment is?" She recalled how the leader, Lux, kept referring to the payment when he first arrived. It seemed to be all they cared about, when they got it, would that mean they would leave? Would Solen?

"Whatever it is, it will be worth it." Calista spun around and smiled at her father who held out his hand to her. "Can a father have this dance with his daughter?"

Rikar and Draken slowly stepped back as Cael led her onto the dance floor. Looking up at her father, Calista felt tears well up in her eyes at the love she saw there.

"You are as lovely as your mother," Cael told her as he swept her around the room, her robe flowing around her. She truly felt like the princess that Rikar and Draken keep calling her. Never had she felt more loved than she did tonight. She was grateful that she had traded in her leather breeches and boots for a light yellow robe that matched her hair.

"NO! You can't have her!"

Calista and Cael jerked around to see Draken with eyes glowing, facing one of the Ancients who had a bored look on his face. Rikar was standing next to his brother with an equally fierce expression while Solen stood between them and the ancient. Her father moved quickly from her side to where his friends stood.

"What is going on, Draken?" he asked but Draken didn't take his eyes from the dispassionate ancient standing there. "Rikar?"

"Tell them," Rikar growled his eyes going dragon. "Tell them what you told us, what you guys are demanding as payment for the breaking of this curse!"

Calista looked over at Solen, who was looking very

torn, but he never moved from his position between the dragons and the Ancients. He looked at her and in his eyes, she saw a struggle that had her heart tightening in her chest.

Calista looked at the ancient standing there, he wasn't one of the ones she had met earlier. As she looked around she saw some of the other Ancients joining their friend, all with the same emotionless expression and white clothing. There weren't many, only eight of them, while the temple was full of Atlanteans, but yet they stood there tall and with no emotion as others started milling around them.

"What is the meaning of this Draken, Rikar?" Tylaos, Malov, and Malis walked up with Lux following, watching everyone.

"Their payment for lifting the curse is Calista!" Draken snarled.

Calista stood there transfixed as she heard his words. She was the payment? She looked around at all the Atlanteans standing there looking as shocked as she was. She had finally found her family, a family who loved her and now she was going to lose them? She saw Brax standing off to the side watching as if an outside observer to a play, which she could suppose he was. He sure didn't care about her.

She turned back where the brothers were not only glaring at the Ancients but also Solen who was still standing in their way.

"Do something, Solen!" they demanded.

"I can't," Solen said tightly.

"Did you know about this?" Cael asked, staring at him.

Solen stared back, his eyes looking hopeless, but it wasn't him that answered, it was Lux. "Solen knew nothing but what his mission was, and that was to bring Calista home and break the curse. There was no need for him to know what payment we required."

"You can't let them take Calista!" Rikar stared at the man both he and Draken had called a friend for so long. Solen only stared back with such a helpless look, it almost broke Calista's heart. Almost. Right now she couldn't get past the part that she was payment for a deal made between her grandparents and the Ancients.

"I would suggest that we adjourn from tonight's festivities," Lux spoke in that controlled manner of his and the other Ancients moved to his side. Solen stayed where he was, staring at Calista, who slowly shook her head.

"You can't take our daughter from us!" Malis beseeched them, but their expressions gave nothing away.

"We'll give you one last week with your daughter, then she will leave with us as payment." Lux nodded to them and moved to leave.

"We won't let you take her!" Draken spoke and his power sparked all around him.

Lux turned to look at him. "We weren't asking permission."

Rikar moved forward. "You'll have to go through us!"

Lux shrugged and turned to Tylaos, Malov, Malis and Cael. "You have one week, then we will come for our payment." He looked right at Calista. "If you try to go back on our deal then you'll not only lose your daughter, but you'll lose your lives as well." He spoke in such a controlled way proclaiming their death as if it was today's special entree. The Ancients then turned and left the temple leaving them all staring, the drink and food forgotten.

CHAPTER 12

"Spider." Solen entered the caves where Calista was trying to process what had happened at the celebration, the Ancients' announcement still ringing in her ears.

"You don't get to call me that!" She whirled on him and the whole room around them shook with her anger. "How could you just stand there after what happened?" Her sympathy had faded from hours earlier, now she was angry. She thought Solen truly cared for her, but it seemed he was only doing as his masters commanded. She didn't care if it sounded selfish, she was feeling selfish.

"Spider... Calista," Solen corrected himself when she raised her arm slightly, energy forming in her hand. "I didn't know what payment they would be asking for, and surely never thought that it would be you."

"So, tell me why you don't seem as shocked about it as the rest of us?" She crossed her arms, closing her hand on the energy ball that had formed. The ball disappeared with a pop that echoed around them ominously.

"Their help usually comes with a price and this isn't the first time it was a person." Solen moved closer.

"But I swear that I didn't know it was going to be you, Calista." He looked at her earnestly.

"Why?" Her voice was harsh with the emotion coursing through her. "If they wanted me so bad, why didn't they just take me?"

"They never just take someone, at least I've never known them to," Solen spoke but at her raised brows he continued, "Which is why when dealing with them, you need to be very clear about any deals made with them, never make a deal without knowing the cost. While they won't just take what they want, they have no problem taking a person as payment," he finished, looking uncomfortable.

Calista glared at him, her hands clenched into fists. "I wasn't the one who made the bargain."

"No, your family was, which makes you as responsible for the bargain as they." Solen moved closer only to draw back when Scratch hissed at him with two legs raised in a threatening manner. "At least in the Ancients' eyes."

"Why be so cruel as to show me what it was like to have a loving family only to take it away? If they had come to me before showing me all this, I would've probably agreed to leave with them just to get away from Ares and the rest of the Greeks." She couldn't stop the tear that escaped and trickled down her cheek. "Why bring me home? Why even tell me about my family here in Atlantis? Why show me what a loving and caring family is just to take it all from me?" Her voice hoarse in her angst.

"I wish I had an answer." Solen stood there looking as lost as she felt.

Scratch hissed up at him but Calista gave a shake of her head. With one last dirty look thrown Solen's way, Scratch scurried across the floor, climbing up her leg to his favorite perch on her shoulder.

Solen watched her with narrowed eyes. "Don't do anything foolish, Calista."

"You don't get to tell me what to do, and neither do your masters," Calista told him before shimmering out of the cave, leaving Solen standing there with a pensive look.

"Hello, granddaughter." Calista took a deep breath hearing Zeus' voice from behind her as she stood looking over the land she had always believed to be her homeland. Not that she could recall very many happy memories, a gentle caress on her neck reminded her they weren't all bad.

"I wasn't looking for company, Grandfather," Calista spoke with a sneer over the last word spoken.

"What have I done to warrant such disrespect?" Zeus asked her, moving to stand in front of her. "Wasn't I the one who gave you your little friend?" He motioned to Scratch, who moved back underneath Calista's hair.

Calista gave a very negligent shake of her head. "And little else."

"I'm not in the habit of fighting the battles of my children or grandchildren." At Calista's sharp bark of laughter Zeus's eyes narrowed.

"Please," she scoffed. "You have intervened numerous times when it suited you."

"Exactly." His chin lifted as he looked down at her. "When it suited me."

Calista's back straightened and her hands clenched. "Thank you."

The puzzled expression on his face would have made her laugh if not for the anger that was coursing through her entire being right now. "For what?" he asked, peering at her intently.

"For reminding me where I stood, I almost forgot how selfish and untrustworthy you Greeks are." Calista didn't raise her voice once, but her words held strength she wasn't aware she had.

"Careful with your words, Granddaughter." Zeus' form started to glow brightly in his rage and grow in size as he stared down at her. "I'll only tolerate so much disrespect."

Calista stared at him, her mouth opening and closing a few times before she gave a short bark of laughter. "You know nothing about disrespect, I have had nothing but disrespect from everyone here!"

"Oh, cry me a river." There on the limb of a tree,

Discord was stretched out staring at Calista with that cruel lift of her lips.

Calista opened her mouth but the loud crack of lightning drowned out whatever she had been about to say. Her hair was blown back from the force of the lightning that struck the ground at Zeus' feet, her eyes closing from the wind that was blowing around. When the wind died down and she opened her eyes, there where Zeus had stood now only a scorched mark remained.

"Hmph." Calista looked up at Discord, who smirked down at her. "Grandfather was always one for the flair." Discord waved her fingers sending several energy jolts towards Calista, making her have to dodge them before falling backwards landing on her ass, staring up at the empty tree limb.

"Ugghhhh!" Calista slammed her hands on the ground as she let out a frustrated shout. The dust kicked up by her hands seemed to float all around her before settling down on her hands. She stood up, shaking the dust off her hands on her leather breeches.

Looking around her at the dusty landscape outside of Olympia, the empty tree and scorch mark on the ground the only indications that anyone else had been there. She really should have known better than to come to Olympia; she had always enjoyed coming here when she was younger to watch the games. Then again, so did the other deities of Greece.

She looked over at the Temple of Zeus, where the

overly ostentatious statue of Zeus resided, with clenched fists. Long ago she looked at him as her only savior in this cruel place she had been brought up in, only to realize he was nothing of the kind.

"You really need to quit letting them get under your skin, Spider." Solen's voice came from the shadows of the columns holding up the entablature of Zeus' temple, and soon she could see Solen appear from the shadows. "Each time you do, they win."

"I don't need any advice from you," she told him through pinched lips. "If it weren't for you…"

"You would still be under Ares' boot believing that you weren't worth anything," Solen finished for her.

"Instead I get to be treated as common currency!" Before he could say anything she shimmered away, leaving him standing there looking aggravated. Something Calista felt he deserved.

Just outside Mitropoleos, Athens there were spectacular gigantic rock formations in the mountains. Mostly untouched by mortals or any of the other deities that roamed Greece. Also, one of Calista's favorite places. There was nothing about this place to entice the others, no glory here, just stone and silence. Perfect for a goddess who wanted to be left alone.

As she traveled over the land of Greece, she was careful to avoid any of the other Greek deities, even those who had been kind to her. Hermes, the ever diligent Messenger of the gods and one who bears many responsibilities, saluted her as he saw her move past him on one of his many treks. She didn't fear him telling anyone about seeing her, while he may be the messenger to the gods, he wasn't one to gossip. That, and he had always liked her.

She saw Aphrodite as she passed through Corinth, but the Goddess of Love paid her no attention, she was too busy with her admirers. Not that Calista wanted her attention; while Aphrodite wasn't as cruel to her as the others, Calista had suffered at her hand as well. As she came closer to her destination, she could hear the forges of Hephaestus off to the distance.

As she appeared on the largest rock formation on the mouth, she looked out at the view over Athens and most of Greece that she could see. It was one that always put her at peace, even during her darkest days. She sat on the ground with one knee propped up and her back against a boulder, one that she lay against many times before.

"Well, if it isn't Ares' daughter, or is it Cael's daughter?"

Calista turned her head to see Alastor, the Greek God of Family Feuds, standing there with that half-cocked smile of his. His skin, darker than any of the other gods or goddesses in Greece, glinted in the sun. Unkempt silver hair which seemed to have a life of its own. It reminded her of Medusa's reptilian locks. Above all of that, one of the few Greek deities who was actually civil to her.

"Hello, Alastor." She nodded to him. "Ares is nothing to me but a bad memory." With those words, she turned away from him, looking out over the view before her rather than the slightly off god. The other gods and goddesses had always given Alastor a wide berth, never caring to have too much to do with him. When she was still speaking to Apollo, he told her of a time when he was at the god's temple and he had "borrowed" a scroll that he saw laying loosely on a shelf. When she had asked what was on the scroll, he told her nothing. At her confused look, he chuckled and informed her that the god was nuttier than Dionysus when he got a bad batch of wine. The scroll contained nonsensical symbols that meant nothing.

Not only did Alastor have his own language that no one but him understood, he also spoke in riddles that made no sense to anyone but himself. Calista had always enjoyed listening to him, even if she didn't know what he was saying. Speaking about glyphs in caves that sing. She loved those stories, used to listen to them and retell them to herself the nights she felt the most alone.

"We both know he is much more than that, little Atlantean Princess," Alastor spoke in that distant like voice of his.

"There is no family squabble here for you to enjoy, Alastor."

"I never did enjoy the fights between you and Ares," he said, moving to sit on a boulder next to her. At her raised brow he chuckled. "Serious as the day is long, I had always hoped to see you put that pompous windbag on his ass."

Calista gave a small lift of a shoulder. "Sorry to disappoint."

"Never said I was disappointed, just that I didn't enjoy the battle." Alastor picked up a pebble from the ground, tossing it in the air and catching it once again. "A battle is nothing when the sides are stacked in one's favor."

Calista said nothing, what he said was nothing but the truth. She knew the odds were always stacked against her when it came to Ares.

"Yes," Alastor continued, examining the pebble in his hand as if it held the answers to life itself. "As long as you were ignorant of whom you truly are, Ares held all the power." The pebble landed in front of Calista with a small thud, kicking up a few dust particles. "Of course, he never really understood the power he had at his fingertips. If he had, I wonder if he would've treated you differently," Alastor mused as he picked up another pebble.

Calista picked up the pebble that he had tossed in front of her. "Alastor, if you have something to say, would you just say it? I'm not in the mood for riddles today. I'm having a real bad day and not in the mood for a family reunion."

This time a scroll landed in her lap, startling her. She turned to look at Alastor who was giving her that lackluster grin of his that made her think the other gods were right about him not being all there in the head. "What is this?"

"The scroll poor Apollo wasn't able to understand, I hoped that he would've let you see it when he was trying to impress you." Alastor gave a dramatic sigh. "But, alas, instead he gave it to Ares, trying to get into his favor." Then he gave a sort of giggle. "Of course, Ares wasn't able to read it either. Neither have the mental capacity of a minotaur."

"What makes you think I can read it if they can't?"

He shrugged. "Open it, don't open it. The choice is yours, but if I was just handed the answer to my questions, I wouldn't waste any time before reading it."

Calista sighed and unrolled the scroll, Alastor gave a gleeful chuckle at her gasp. She turned to him. "You're Atlantean!"

CHAPTER 13

m I?" Alastor's face split into the crazed grin she remembered well, the one that had others giving him a wide berth.

She looked down at the scroll in her hands then back up at him, her eyes bright and her smile almost as wide as his, "I can read this." Looking back down at the scroll she started to read while Alastor watched her smiling as he kicked his feet against the boulder. He gave a mad little chuckle when her eyes widened at what she was reading. Calista looked up at him tilting her head a bit. "Is this the scroll the traitor took from Atlantis?"

Alastor let out a peal of laughter that reverberated off the stone around them, his face showing his glee, a glee that Calista wasn't sure she understood. "You could say that." He leaned his head to the side, his eyes starting to glaze over over with that faraway look he was known for.

"How did you end up with it?"

Alastor looked down at her, his eyes bright with either madness or glee, possibly both knowing him. "Are you sure you're ready to hear that?"

Calista sighed. "Alastor, no games. I'm tired of games, tired of riddles and really tired of surprises."

Alastor pushed himself up off the rock until he was merely a few feet above it, crossed his legs then let himself slowly descend till he was now sitting on the boulder cross legged. "You should be happy, little princess."

"Why do you say that?"

"You know who you are, you know you have a family that loves you. Wouldn't that make anyone happy?" Alastor placed his elbows on his knees, pressing his wrists together so that his hands created a rest for his chin that he now placed in the center.

"They are wanting to take me away, Alastor, away from my family," Calista told him.

"They?" His silver hair flying in the breeze as he turned to look at her, lifting his chin from his palms that moved to rest on his knees, his eyes wide and full of curiosity.

"The Ancients." Calista's voice hardened at even saying their name.

For the first time since Calista could remember, Alastor's face cleared up so that there wasn't a trace of the madness that normally shone all around him. He looked sane, even his silver mane seemed to settle peacefully against his scalp. "The Ancients have shown their hand already …" His voice drifted off as his eyes went from clear to distant.

Calista waved her hand in front of his face. "Alastor!"

She said his name sharply to get his attention. She even snapped her fingers. "Hey!"

Alastor's eyes slowly came back into focus and he moved his head to look at her, his look no longer one of insanity but one of calculation. Calista wasn't sure which expression was worse. "What are the Ancients after?"

Calista frowned, "Didn't you hear me? Me!" she told him, her hands wide in her aggravation.

Alastor looked at her, his fingers moving to pull on the silver strands of his beard thoughtfully. "They aren't demanding anything or anyone else for you?"

Her brow furrowed at his question, he may look as if he is sane right now but those questions were making her doubt that. "No, they want me as payment for breaking the curse and bringing me home."

"They broke the curse?"

"Well … no, I did when I crossed the barrier, but since Solen was the one who brought me to Atlantis under their orders, they are asking for me in payment."

"Asking?" Alastor raised a brow. "If they are asking, just say no."

Calista sighed, "Well, either I go with them, or Atlantis goes to war with them."

"Ahhh." Alastor raised his head high. "So they are demanding, not asking," he said slowly nodding his head. "That sounds more like them."

"You know them?" Calista asked.

"Be careful listening to this fool, Spider." Calista twirled around, her eyes narrowing as she saw Solen standing there in his long cloak. Solen wasn't looking at her, instead he was staring at Alastor with an intense look. One the insane god barely acknowledged as he looked over at Solen, his sane smile going back to one of insanity.

"You must be the messenger of the Ancients that has our little princess upset," Alastor spoke, his voice full of amusement as Solen's eyes narrowed on him.

"She isn't your anything, you fool." Calista's eyes narrowed at the curt tone, it was as if Solen despised Alastor. She looked between the two, not sure what was going on between them.

"Oh?" Alastor continued to look at Solen with amusement. "Is she yours?"

"I belong to no one!" Calista bit out before they could get into an argument over something they were both wrong about.

Solen took a deep breath and tore his gaze from Alastor. "I'm sorry, Spider, I just worry about what nonsense this fool is trying to fill your head when you already have enough to worry about."

"Fool, am I?" Alastor asked him, leaning towards him, his fingers intertwining as he stared at Solen. "Afraid what I will tell her, Champion?"

Solen started towards him, but Calista's words stopped him. "Champion? I thought you said you were a Hunter?"

Alastor's eyes lit up at her words, his eyes never leaving Solen, who was starting to look uncomfortable. "So, you are the Ancients' great hunter? The one who never fails."

"Keep speaking your nonsense and I'll show you how this Hunter can rid you of that foul tongue." Solen glared at Alastor but he only chortled with glee.

"Nonsense? Why is it nonsense to want to actually tell me what is going on rather than keeping me in the dark until it's too late?" Honestly, Calista did have to agree with Solen about Alastor speaking nonsense, but she would be damned if she admitted it to him.

"Spider—" Solen started but she interrupted him.

"Don't call me that!" The air around them crackled with energy. Something Alastor noticed with glee while Calista barely paid any attention, she was staring at Solen who was looking cautiously around then back at her, holding up a placating hand.

"Fine, Calista," he spoke calmly. "You need to be careful listening to him." He motioned towards Alastor who was now standing on the ground leaning against the boulder that he had been sitting on with his legs crossed, looking amused as he watched them both. Calista knew Alastor loved a good feud, he was the God of Family Feuds after all.

"Why?" She decided to ignore Alastor and focus on Solen; she was still angry at him but right now her need for answers outweighed her anger.

"Because he's still bitter for being rejected by the Ancients so many years ago and is just using you to fuel his revenge." Solen started to move forward, but she held up a hand, bringing him to a stop with a sigh.

She looked at Alastor. "Is this true, were you rejected by the Ancients?"

Alastor tilted his head a bit, as if contemplating the question, then gave a shrug before responding simply, "Yes."

Calista felt confused as she just shook her head, not understanding any of this. She looked at Alastor. "You wanted to be with the Ancients? Why?"

"To be a Champion of the Ancients is better than being royalty," Alastor told her, not moving from his relaxed leaning position as his head nodded towards Solen. "Ask loverboy here, when you work for the Ancients you can do anything you want to do. As long as you come running when they call." The last was said with a sneer.

"Better than being a librarian in charge of Atlantean lore," Solen shot back at him.

"And yet this librarian had something the Ancients wanted... badly." Alastor looked at the scroll in Calista's hand, bringing Solen's attention to it. Calista moved the scroll to hide it within the folds of her tunic, keeping it there by the leather belt she wore around her waist. "Although, I think this time I might have dodged a bullet."

"You're forgetting something, old man." Solen's voice was so cold that Calista was sure she could feel a frost forming. Alastor raised a brow at him, Solen's next words had her body freezing. "Why don't you tell Calista who was the one who delivered her to Ares that night?" He practically dared Alastor, who gave a slight shrug.

Calista looked over at Alastor, swallowing hard. "You betrayed your own people, you stole the scroll from its place in the archives, and you are the reason that I grew up under the boot of Ares? How could you?"

Alastor turned his hard stare onto her. "You don't think I haven't been punished? I haven't been able to return home thanks to the curse that was put on Atlantis. Being away from my temple has turned my mind against me. No god or goddess can stay away from their temple for too long without losing a bit of themselves. I have been punished for my crimes, princess, trust me."

"I don't understand how you can justify betraying your family and friends just for power. A power that makes you practically a slave to the Ancients. You are a god, wasn't that enough power for you?" Calista stared right back into his hardened gaze.

Alastor gave a grunt and shrugged. "What can I say? When they came to offer Brax's wife a place amongst their ranks, the idea appealed to me." Calista's eyes widened hearing him say Brax had a wife so carelessly, but he continued speaking. "I approached them about joining them but they weren't interested until they discovered I was the keeper of all the scrolls of Atlantis. Any prophecy that was spoken, any story told and all the history of Atlantis was in my archives. That, they were interested in."

"Not enough to take your treacherous hide to their home," Solen told him with disgust.

Alastor turned to him. "Oh, your precious masters would have taken me with them when they left in exchange for one certain scroll."

Calista frowned. "Wait, then why didn't you go?" She was having a hard time following this conversation and she wasn't sure if it was because of Alastor's insanity or because the conversation itself made no sense.

Alastor turned his head to look at her. "Let's just say a little birdie informed me that the Ancients; plans for me weren't as grand as I was led to believe. They had no place for me among the Champions but there are always places in the servants quarters."

"You're telling me they could turn a god into a servant?" Calista couldn't wrap her mind around that.

"If I would have stepped onto their ship willingly? Yes," Alastor told her. "Thankfully, I had the sense to trust the information and disappear with the scroll so the Ancients couldn't get their hands on it." He cast his eyes down, "I regret I had already handed you to Ares when I discovered this."

"It was a fate more than you deserved," Solen told him, his voice dripping with contempt.

"Solen!" Calista frowned at him.

He looked at her. "How can you defend what this man did? He stole you from your family and barely shows remorse."

She stared back at him. "How is that different from what you are doing? I don't see you standing up to the Ancients, telling them that I'm off limits."

"Woohoo!" Alastor chortled. "She got you there boy—ooof!" Solen moved swiftly, so swiftly Calista hadn't even realized he moved until he was there, pressing his elbow into Alastor's windpipe, holding the god against the boulder he had been leaning upon.

"Want to test if one of the Ancients' Champions can kill a god?"

Solen practically spat into his face as he pushed harder against Alastor who looked as if he was having a hard time breathing. Calista expected Alastor to disappear and leave Solen there empty handed but the god just stood there, his hands not even rising to protect him from Solen as he pressed against his throat.

"So, how is Brax?" Alastor asked, something that stumped Calista some more. She truly wasn't understanding this conversation or their actions at all. "Is he being a good little boy and doing what your masters are telling him to do?" Now that caught Calista's attention.

"Shut up, you crazy coot!" Solen bit out between his teeth.

"What is he talking about, Solen?" Calista kept looking between the two of them.

"You should ask loverboy about Brax's wife." Alastor started to laugh but it was cut off when Solen pressed even harder on his throat.

"Shut up!" Solen screamed, slamming Alastor against the boulder so hard if Alastor had been a normal man, he would surely be dead.

Alastor grinned. "What's wrong? Don't want the princess to know how you have been lying to her and manipulating her for your masters?" Alastor looked over at Calista, who was watching them both with wide eyes, then back at Solen, who had stepped back and was pulling out his sword. "I think I'm done now." With a crack the god was gone, just as Solen plunged his sword, intent on skewering the lunatic god.

"What was he talking about?" Calista asked Solen again.

"Nothing!" Solen told her, sheathing his sword but she grabbed his arm and jerked him around to face her.

"Is what he said true? That you have been lying and manipulating me?" she asked him.

"Calista, you don't understand—" He attempted to reason with her but she was beyond that as she shook her head interrupting him.

"Is it?" Her voice rose.

"Yes!" he yelled at her, drowning her out. His face looked defeated and full of angst, but that one word felt worse than all the slaps and kicks Ares had given her in her whole life. "Calista," he implored her as he reached out to her but she backed away from him.

"Don't!" she told him, holding up her hand. "Leave me alone!" With that she shimmered from there, wanting to be away from everyone. As the view around her started to shimmer and break apart, she heard Solen right before she disappeared.

"Dammit, Spider!"

CHAPTER 14

Trying to get away from everyone, Calista came to the site where Atlantis had stood proud above the water before the curse that sent her home below the waves. Far from Greece, in the middle of the Aegean sea, nestled within the walls of an island whose arms once cradled the great city but now were empty.

She had only been home for a short time, but even in that little bit of time she felt so much more love than she had her whole lifetime. She saw how a family should be, how gods and goddesses could actually work with the mortals that worshiped them. When Malis had caught Ares' eye and been spurned, that was the only crime committed. Their world sentenced to imprisonment deep in the ocean, the Atlantean deities all worked together to protect the mortals of their land.

In Atlantis, the mortals worked with the deities in keeping their world safe. Maybe not all, she wrinkled her nose thinking about Brax. But even he didn't deserve the punishment that was inflicted on her people, nor did he deserve to lose his wife. The mortals of Atlantis were great thinkers, philosophers and scientists with advanced thoughts so far ahead of their time. The deities there complimented them, except for her. She was a goddess of nothing, as Discord liked to remind her.

"So, you're the one the Ancients want."

The air around Calista crackled as she straightened and turned to face the soft spoken, raven haired female who stood there, gazing at her with such interest. She didn't wear the robes of the gods nor the Chitons that most mortals wore. Her dress reminded Calista of the blue silk that she saw back in Atlantis with golden hemming. An ivory belt adorned her waist, knotted in the center with pearl-like ribbons flowing down to knee length.

"Who are you?" Calista was sure she had never seen her in Greece, and was pretty sure she hadn't seen her in Atlantis either.

"I guess you can say I'm the reason the Ancients want you so badly." The girl spoke softly and so matter-of-factly, Calista was momentarily speechless. "Well, my mother actually, but since she passed, I guess I now carry her blame."

"Your mother?"

The girl nodded and moved elegantly past Calista, her blue folds swaying with each movement as she looked down at the watery emptiness where Atlantis once stood. A look in her eyes of such emotion that it made Calista swallow hard. "My mother started all the events that have happened since that fateful day. She carried the burden until her death just a few years back." The girl gave a soft sigh. "And now the burden is mine."

"Wait!" Calista moved closer to her, peering down at her. "Why would your mother start such atrocities? What did the Atlanteans do to her?"

The girl turned her sea green eyes on Calista, there was a perpetual sadness there that made it hard for Calista to be angry with her. "She was Atlantean."

"I don't understand," Calista dropped down onto the cliff, letting her leg hang over the side.

The girl moved closer, daintily lowering herself till she sat close to Calista on the cliff. "My name is Shaylane, my mother's name was Trelaine, and she was the Atlantean Goddess of Vision and Circumstance, wife to Brax."

Calista's eyes widened and her words frozen in her throat as her mind attempted to process what Shaylane was telling her. It took her a few moments, and Shaylane sat there more patient than she could've been while she took her time to collect her thoughts and put her words together.

"You're Brax's daughter?" Even after pausing a few minutes before speaking, that was the only thing Calista could come up with.

Shaylane sat there quietly looking forward and Calista gave a silent groan, she might have just put her foot in her mouth. "Uh—"

"Yes."

Calista stopped what she was saying, she barely heard the softly spoken word, wasn't even sure she heard her right. "What?"

"Yes, I'm Brax's daughter," Shaylane told her. "My mother was pregnant when she agreed to leave with the Ancients."

"Why did she agree to leave with them?" Calista couldn't imagine why a mother would take a child from their father, even one as arrogant as Brax.

"To save my father."

Calista stared at her, eyes wide at her words.

"My mother made sure to tell me the story so that I would know my father didn't abandon us." The words were softly spoken, but so much emotion was evident. Not once did Shaylane look away from the empty water before them. For the first time since Calista had come to Atlantis she felt sympathy for Brax, not that she thought he would want it.

"The Ancients came to Atlantis all those years ago, when Atlantis was still bathed in the warmth of the sun, searching for the one who could finally free them from their oppressors." Shaylane looked up into the sun, closing her eyes as if enjoying a caress from a loved one. Calista wondered if this was the first time she had ever seen the sun.

"The Ancients have oppressors?" Calista interrupted her then instantly felt a twinge of guilt. "Sorry."

Shaylane gave a small smile. "It's all right, and yes

the Ancients have oppressors, someone they fear. With good reason."

"Who are these oppressors?" Calista's mind was churning with this new information, what if these oppressors of the Ancients could help her out of her situation.

"A race of beings that the Ancients tried to enslave, and why they are so careful with the ones they... acquire now."

"Do you think they would help us now?" Calista started to feel a glimmer of hope, a glimmer that faded at the small shake of Shaylane's dark locks.

"I've never encountered any of the Criptines. What I do know is the Ancients have been running from them since the Criptines destroyed their home world in retaliation for what they did," Shaylane smoothed out a wrinkle that Calista couldn't see in her dress. "The Ancients believed themselves to be gods with no weaknesses. The Criptines proved them wrong."

"Where is the Ancients' new home?" Calista asked.

Shaylane looked up into the clear sky above them, "Since that day, the Ancients gathered what was left of their homeworld as well as the survivors and have been traveling through the stars on a large spaceship created from what was left of their home world. They don't dare to stay in one place for too long of a time lest the Criptines, who are still hunting for them, find them." A small smile started to form as she continued to speak.

"After the Ancients gathered the survivors and enough of their world to create their new nomadic home, they discovered that very few of their slaves survived the destruction. So they ran, going from star system to star system, looking for new slaves to serve them, this time they were also looking for more powerful beings that would protect them from the Criptines."

"Criptines? That is the race of the ones the Ancients fear?" Shaylane nodded at Calista's question. "Are they gods as well?"

Shaylane's lips pursed as she stared up at the sky. "The Ancients called them parasites but my mother believed they were gods."

"Will they help us?" she wondered again.

A sigh slipped from Shaylane's lips. "I wouldn't even know where to begin to look for them. I've never met one and not sure if I would even survive if I did."

"If we can't seek them out for help, is there any way for us to defeat the Ancients without me losing my freedom?" Calista just found a family that loved her, she wasn't ready to give it up.

"I believe my mother left a clue on how to defeat them before she left her home all those years ago." Shaylane looked over at Calista, her eyes moving down to where the scroll Calista had hidden was resting.

"Why were the Ancients after your mother?"

"As I said, my mother was the Atlantean Goddess of Vision and Circumstance. She could not only see the future but also the different circumstances that could change that future." Calista could hear the pride in her voice as she spoke of her mother. She had to swallow the envy she felt deep inside. "As I said before, the Ancients were acquiring powerful beings that could be used to protect them from multiple star systems, some were willing, some were bargained for and others were acquired through immoral means."

Calista swallowed a lump that formed in her throat, realizing that is exactly what the Ancients were attempting to do to her, acquire her as if she was a possession.

When Calista stayed silent, Shaylane continued, "One of their willing Champions who also had the power of vision, although he wasn't able to control his vision to create multiple outcomes, but he did see that the way to defeating the Criptines was on a distant planet called Earth."

"Your mother?" Calista frowned when Shaylane shook her head.

"No, but the Champion had lost his life in a battle with a Criptine hunting party before they made it to this star system. His dying words were telling the Ancients that there was another on Earth who could see as he could." A shoulder lifted slightly. "Of course, they never did truly understand my mother and her powers."

"What do you mean?"

"My mother could see multiple futures as well as change them to see what consequence would happen due to that change. Something the original Champion of sight couldn't do, and something my mother never brought to their attention. They arrived in Atlantis to try to convince my mother to become their new Champion of Sight. She turned them down."

"I take it they didn't take the rejection well," Calista stated more than she asked, Shaylane gave a sad nod.

"When she refused, they turned their attention to others in Atlantis, making implications about destroying Atlantis if she didn't leave with them. The gods and goddesses of Atlantis were ready to fight for my mother rather than let the Ancients take her." Shaylane ran a finger through the sand on the ground next to her. "They gave my mother a week, and during that week Atlantis readied for war."

"I didn't read any of that in the historical scrolls," Calista tilted her head to the side. "And if they had done that once before, why would my grandparents and parents dare to reach out to them again?"

"During that week, my mother spent much of the time in her visions, to see if there was a way that the Ancients could be defeated." Shaylane's finger lifted the sand and let it trickle through her fingers. "What she saw was the destruction of Atlantis, so she decided to leave with the Ancients as long as they spared her home."

"That doesn't explain why anyone from Atlantis would reach out to them to bring me home after that."

Shaylane gave her an apologetic look. "My mother

saw the only way to defeat them was to create the circumstances in which you ended up growing up in Greece and Atlantis was cursed to the bottom of the sea. She made sure the Ancients knew no one in Atlantis could remember what happened."

Calista felt as if she had been punched in the gut, now she understood why Shaylane said her mother was responsible, she really was. "I'm not sure I understand this, why would your mother want to curse Atlantis?"

"Shaylane!"

Looking over her shoulder Calista saw two muscular warriors standing there, the female giving Calista a curious look while the male had his arms crossed looking very foreboding. "Time for you to head back to your room."

Calista rose swiftly in defense of Shaylane who just smiled at the pair, her voice holding no greeting, "You don't have permission to be here, musclehead."

The male didn't even spare her a glance as he stood there in a warrior's armor that would've made Ares green with jealousy. His chest plate covered every vital area in bright silver with a gold emblem covered in red rubies and yellow topaz stones in a very intricate design. On his back was the scabbard for an ornate looking sword while he wore leather breeches and boots with the same intricate armor overlapping key sensitive areas. She had half a mind to see if that armor did indeed protect those areas, but a raise of the man's brow told her he was watching her as carefully as the woman next to him.

"Shaylane, we need to go before your absence is discovered." The male spoke arrogantly to Shaylane as if Calista hadn't even spoken. Something Calista wasn't about to let slide as she opened her mouth to remind muscles she was standing right there when Shaylane laid a gentle hand on her arm and gave a small shake of her head.

Shaylane then turned to look at the warriors, no fear in her eyes as she spoke to them, "There is still much she needs to know."

The female stepped forward and spoke, her voice masculine and deep. "Let her figure it out herself, you are playing with fire being gone this long."

Shaylane looked at the woman. "I thought playing with fire was your job."

"Listen to Clori." The male inclined his head towards his female companion, reprimanding Shaylane's words in his voice. "She is only looking out for you, little one."

Shaylane smiled up at him. "I know, Clay, and I do appreciate it but if my mother were here—"

"If your mother were here," Clay interrupted her, "then she would tell the female as much as she needed to know to start her on her journey, as you've done and then let the female do what she must."

Shaylane sighed then looked at Calista. "My mother told the Ancients you were the key to finding this great power they seek, she told me that you're not only the key to this great power but also the key to defeating the Ancients once and for all."

Calista reached for Shaylane's hand as she went to move away, an action that had the two warriors tensing. A lift of Shaylane's hand had them staying their ground but their posture never softened. "Shaylane," Calista implored her. "I know nothing about how to find a key or a great power, I'm kind of a failure at being a goddess." The last was said softly as Calista lowered her eyes after admitting the deepest fear she had always held so close to her.

Shaylane put her hand under Calista's chin and lifted her head up, the two warriors that stood behind Shaylane no longer tense as they gazed at Calista with sympathetic eyes. "You were never a failure, Calista, your power has lain dormant within you all these years, only showing itself at times of great need."

"Well, I don't think there is a greater need than right now."

Shaylane smiled at Calista's words. "Your power is there within you, this power will make you one of the most powerful deities in Atlantis, all you have to do is accept who you are."

"Who am I?"

"The Atlantis Goddess of Manipulation."

Clay moved forward, placing his hand on Shaylane's shoulder. "Enough, now she must figure it out on her own." With a curt nod to Calista, the air around the trio started to glow so brightly that Calista had to cover her eyes. When she moved her hands and looked around, they were gone.

CHAPTER 15

Calista looked around her, how many times had she come here when she was younger not knowing what had drawn her here? The site of where Ares stole her in the middle of the night right before sending her family and the people of Atlantis to the bottom of the sea, all because her mother rejected Ares' advances.

"Who knew that being faithful was a crime?" she muttered out loud, looking down into the watery depths thinking about her family and what they must be going through right now. They had waited all these years to be free, waited for her and now all because they were willing to fight for her, they faced annihilation from gods from the stars.

In Greece she was considered a failure as a diety and now she was about to be the cause of her family's destruction.

"Come wunning home to dadda?" The mocking voice of Discord had her back straightening as her body tensed.

Turning, she saw Discord standing there in her signature dark locks and black leather. Calista stared at

Discord and smiled, a smile that widened when Discord's eyes narrowed. "If I remember correctly, I learned at a young age that running to Ares was as useless as a hairbrush in your hands." Discord's eyes bulged at that comment. Aphrodite was forever making fun of how her hair was always unkempt in front of Ares, who would chuckle. While Ares may favor Discord, he would do nothing to upset Aphrodite.

The frustrated shriek that came from Discord's lips had birds scattering to the air around them but Calista stood there watching her, no sign of amusement in her eyes even though she hit a bullseye. Calista knew better than to let her guard down around Discord. That lesson had not only been painful each time, but embarrassing most times considering it usually came from a more powerful source.

Just as that thought ran through her mind she could feel the energy coming from behind her. Pushing off the ground, she flipped through the air to land several feet away from the scorched ground where Ares' energy blast had landed, exactly where she had stood only moments before.

"Coming to your pet's rescue as always, Ares," Calista spoke, staring straight at him, fighting down the butterflies that were swarming around in her gut. Never in her life had she ever been able to avoid his energy blasts or any of his attacks.

The look of disbelief on his face helped to quell some

of those butterflies and even give her esteem a bit of a boost. Although she knew not to get too cocky or she could lose this tentative upper hand that she acquired. "You could have learned a lot from Discord, but instead you failed and became nothing more than a disgrace." Ares sneered at her.

Calista snorted. "What? Learned how to come running when you whistled, like a trained dog? No thanks, I like having a mind of my own."

"Why you!" Discord moved to attack her, but Ares held up his hand, effectively halting her, which brought a sneer from Calista.

"Did you forget you needed permission from your master before attempting to play with the big girls?" Calista wasn't sure where this was coming from, but it felt good. It also angered Discord so much that she launched herself at Calista, who was ready for her. Ares shouted but Discord was so enraged she either didn't hear him or didn't care.

The air around Calista started to move as Calista watched Discord moving as if in slow motion towards her. She moved her body slightly to the right, creating a wall in the air where she had once stood, a wall that encased Discord within its embrace. Her eyes widened as she looked at Calista, the realization that she had underestimated the goddess she had once bullied shining brightly in her eyes.

Calista walked towards her as she struggled against

the invisible binds. "Once, you were able to bully me and I now realize that only happened because I allowed it. That ends now! I'm no longer that scared and lonely little goddess. And I'm no longer scared of you." Calista was staring right into her eyes, merely inches away as she finished those words. "You may be the Goddess of Chaos, but I'm the Goddess of Manipulation, and that trumps you."

Discord continued to struggle, her hatred shining in her eyes as she let out a strangled scream. She wasn't surprised when Discord disappeared with a snap from view, she knew Ares would come to her rescue but she had made her point. She turned with a smirk, enjoying the glare Discord sent her way and the look of irritation Ares gave her.

For most of her life she had lived in fear of the other Greek gods and goddesses who always looked down on her with disdain and treated her as if she were a mere bug to be stepped on. For the first time, she felt as if the tables had turned and she had no plans on letting them get the upper hand again.

"You'll never trump me, you'll always be an insignificant bug whose only friend is another insignificant bug." Ares sneered at her with Discord standing behind him, giving her haughty looks with her chin raised.

Calista stared at him with raised brows, not believing what he was saying. "Are you serious?" she spoke, her words full of sardonic laughter. "I'm not the one hiding behind anyone, I'm standing on my own two feet facing you both. You are no longer facing a defenseless child."

"Careful, bug, or I'll rip your tongue out and feed it to your pet bug," Ares practically growled at her.

Calista snorted, "You are nothing more than a coward Ares, I'm no longer scared of you."

The look on Ares' face gave her a bit of satisfaction as she could see the redness appear in his olive colored skin, so much that his face was glowing brightly in his anger. Calista tensed as she waited for the backlash from her bravado. When his eyes cleared of the anger, the redness receded and a smile appeared she stepped back, watching him warily. Out of all things she expected, it surely wasn't that.

"You may no longer be scared of me, but I bet you can't say the same for him," Ares gave a malicious grin as he nodded her way before grabbing Discord and disappearing from sight.

Whirling around in the direction of Ares' nod, she saw one of the Ancients standing there, the sun glinting off of his silver skin and clothing. Her stomach knotted and her hands clenched. At least Ares and Discord had left so they couldn't enjoy her discomfort. "What do you want?" she spoke, her throat tight as she tried to hide her apprehension and stand tall.

"You know what we want. You," he said plainly.

"I'm not a possession for you to take," she told him,

swallowing hard as she tried to not show her fear. She had just faced down Ares and Discord, no way could she fold now.

The Ancient gave a smile that didn't show his teeth, a sly one that told her he noticed all that she attempted to hide from him. He started moving towards her, the smile widening just slightly as she stepped back from him. "That is exactly what you are."

"The girl said she wasn't interested, Lars," came a masculine voice from behind her, one that wasn't familiar to her at all. Turning around she saw a male with flowing yellow locks that would make Aphrodite jealous, standing there in full silver and blue armor that glinted in the sun. A sword of glowing blue in his hand and a silver shield with the same blue glow shining brightly as well.

"This isn't your business, Vlan," the Ancient told him, not taking his eyes off Calista as he still moved towards her.

"I refuse to stand idly by as you attempt to tear another from their world for your selfish whims," Vlan told him, moving closer to Calista with his sword still drawn.

"Take care, Champion, and remember where your loyalties lie." The Ancient paused in his stride, turning his gaze from Calista to Vlan.

With a flash of light, Vlan moved from his position to stand in front of Calista. "Enough of your silver tongue, Lars." The air around Vlan filled with energy that radiated from his armor, sword and shield. "Leave this place and go back to your ship."

"You dare challenge me?" Lars straightened and seemed to grow before their eyes but Vlan stayed his ground in front of Calista. Never had she had someone try to protect her, she didn't know how to act, so she just stood there and watched the Ancient before them as he narrowed his eyes at Vlan.

"You're making a huge mistake," Lars told him.

"The only mistake I made was in not standing up to you when you came to my world, a mistake I won't make again."

Lars' eyes narrowed, "This isn't the end of this." With those words, the air around the Ancient started to glow brightly, causing them to cover their eyes. When they could see once more, the Ancient was gone.

Vlan turned to Calista, "You must hurry home, a war is brewing and they need you."

"Th-thank you," Calista said slowly. The words and the Champion's actions were so alien to her it took her a moment to think of what to say.

Vlan nodded, "You're welcome, see you back in Atlantis." With those words he was gone, leaving her standing there, looking at the empty space.

Calista was about to shimmer down to Atlantis when

she felt the scroll she had hidden in her tunic. Grabbing the scroll she unrolled it and finished reading. The scroll spoke of gods coming from the stars, gods that take the power they want and if they aren't stopped they will enslave all. To find the key to defeating them a path must be followed.

A mother of vision must leave with the gods to the stars to start the journey, leaving behind a clue to the one who will finally free all those imprisoned by the gods and their trickery. An uncle will betray his family and a civilization will fall to bring the key to unlock the prison doors.

The edge of the scroll was decorated with glyphs that looked vaguely familiar to her and at the very end was a prophecy. This prophecy looked to be written in handwriting different from the rest of the scroll, while the ink looked a darker color than the other writing as well. It was centered and looked like it had been hurriedly written down.

"To bring about the fall of the false gods, one goddess must be awakened and another freed. To win, the sleepwalker must manipulate the odds, only then will the prophecy succeed." Calista frowned, this made no sense to her.

"The gods from the stars must be the Ancients and the mother of vision has to be Shaylane's mother," Calista murmured to herself. She still couldn't wrap her mind around the fact that Shaylane is Brax's daughter and once he had a wife. She wasn't sure who the one imprisoned was or even the uncle who had betrayed his family.

She wondered if the civilization that fell was Atlantis, although it didn't truly fall. She paused, her brow furrowing slightly, "Unless it means their fall beneath the waves." She wasn't sure how she felt about her true home being prophesied to be submerged in the ocean. If Shaylane's mother knew that was going to happen then why didn't she warn someone? Why would she start the events to help that happen? "There has to be more to this than... this!" She clenched the scroll in her hand, looking down into the depths down below. "Time to go home." With those words, she shimmered from her position.

CHAPTER 16

She wasn't sure what she expected when she shimmered into the center of Atlantis, looking around her at all the activity, she was sure this wasn't even close. Her eyes wide as she looked around not only at the Atlanteans gearing up for war but also people she had no idea who they were. The greatest shock though, she couldn't deny, was the Greek gods and demigods that were dressing in their battle finery as well.

"Princess!" She turned to see a smiling Rikar coming her way, looking as handsome as always. His armor of Atlantean design, practical and yet stylish enough to be able to give him freedom of movement. He held his helmet to his side by his arm. "Wondered if you were going to join the party."

"Party?" She looked around her still not sure exactly what was going on. "What's going on?"

"A war, Spider." She whirled to see Solen standing there with Vlan, she was momentarily stunned by the sight of Solen in actual armor. Gone was his long tunic and odd breeches with leather boots. In place his legs were clad not only in armor, but Atlantean armor, arms were well protected as well and there on his chest was a golden spider. Just like Rikar, the armor was not only practical, but stylish as well.

"What are you doing here?" Finally she got her voice back as she stared at him.

"He's here to help us fight the Ancients, Calista." She turned and there stood Draken and her father, both in Atlantean armor. She ran and hugged her father, who wrapped his arms around her. "My little girl." He kissed her temple then smiled at her. "Solen is joining us in our battle against the Ancients, he was in their service when he came here, but now he is fighting against them."

Calista gave her father a smile, then turned to Solen as she moved from her father's embrace. "That's all good and well, but where were you when the Ancients came for me above?" She pointed up. "You surely didn't come to my aid then."

"Solen was the one who sent me," Vlan spoke up.

Calista frowned at him. "Why you?"

But it was Solen who answered. "I didn't think you would accept help from me."

Calista looked down, she couldn't deny his words, it hadn't been that long since she told him to stay away from her. She pursed her lips, not sure what to say.

"Spider." She looked up into Solen's gaze as he stood before her. "I can't take back what I have done, all I can do now is try to make up for it." His hand moved to hold her cheek. "If you let me."

Her tongue darted out to moisten her lips, looking away to gather her thoughts before responding. "Well, you're already dressed for battle." She shrugged.

Rikar and her father chuckled, "That's my girl."

She looked up and smiled at her father before turning to Solen. "Win this battle and then we can talk."

He gave a cocky grin, "I will hold you to that." She nodded at him and turned to see her mother walking up to her in full armor. Calista decided she definitely liked the Atlantean armor more than the heavy and bulky Greek armor she had grown up around.

"Are you joining us in battle, my daughter?" Malis smiled proudly at Calista, who nodded. Malis turned to her acolytes who were always in attendance. "Gather armor for my daughter. We have a battle to win."

Calista followed the young red-haired acolyte in her light blue robes as she moved through the busy trails running between the temples and buildings of Atlantis. As they moved Calista looked around her and was amazed at what she saw.

Atmos, the God of Wisdom and Arts, was suiting up in the Atlantean armor along with Stratos. Brine was also suiting up while her acolytes, who could be seen readying the medical supplies. When Brine herself put on some armor, Calista looked at her mother's acolyte. "Is Brine fighting? Shouldn't she stay behind to help with the wounded?"

The acolyte smiled at her. "The Goddess Brine has trained her acolytes well and has made it known that she refused to stay behind while her family goes off to possibly the bloodiest battle of our lives."

Calista nodded, she understood that feeling all too well. "Wait!" Calista stopped and looked back to where the trio stood, the acolyte paused and waited patiently for Calista to tell her why they stopped, "I thought Stratos was neutral in all things?"

The acolyte nodded. "The God Stratos is neutral, being the God of Law and Justice he needs to be, but in this battle there is no place for neutrality. Atlantis is under the threat of annihilation if we don't win."

The knot in Calista's stomach tightened at her words; this war was because of her. Her family was fighting and risking their lives for her.

She didn't realize that her emotions were showing until the acolyte gasped and was quick to reassure her. "This isn't your fault Goddess Calista, please don't think that."

"The acolyte is correct, Calista." They turned and there stood Shaylane smiling at her, Brax in full Atlantean armor standing next to his daughter. "This war was foretold long before your birth, my mother played her part in this war, and now you must play your part."

Calista gave a snort, "I just wish I knew what my part is."

"When it is time, you will know." Shaylane smiled at her. "Until then, we will all fight to protect not only our loved ones but others from becoming slaves to the Ancients."

"You'll stay behind," Brax informed her in that no argument allowed voice of his. "I lost you once, I won't lose you again."

Shaylane turned to look up at Brax, he was after all several feet taller than her, "I'll join in the battle Father, I'll not sit on the sidelines while my family fights for their freedom. Mother not only trained my powers, but my fighting ability as well, she wouldn't want me to sit on the sidelines. She didn't sacrifice everything she had to have her daughter hide." Her words weren't loud, weren't mean, but they were absolute.

Calista looked at Brax, wondering what he was going to do, even in her short time here in Atlantis she knew he hated his words being challenged. She just wasn't sure if that extended to his daughter as well.

Brax stared at his daughter with a stern look for a few more minutes then, for the first time since she met him, Calista saw a smile start to emerge. "You are your mother's daughter." With those words he pulled her into his arms for an embrace.

Calista smiled, it seemed Brax did have a soft spot, at least for his daughter.

Brax turned his attention to Calista, the smile gone from just a few moments ago. "See you on the battlefield, Goddess of Manipulation."

Calista's eyes widened as she looked at Shaylane, who smiled. "You will know when." With those cryptic words, father and daughter walked off.

Watching them walk away she got another shock, there were Greek gods and goddesses here as well, suiting up in their heavy and clunky Greek armor. She turned to the still smiling acolyte who responded, "We have allies for this fight, the Ancients have underestimated us all. When life as we know it becomes threatened, old wounds need to be addressed later, we must join together to preserve both our worlds. The Greeks know if they stand idly by while we fight for our freedom then there is no guarantee theirs won't be next."

Calista nodded as they came to her mother's temple where she followed the acolyte inside. "What's your name?" Calista asked as they moved to her mother's inner chambers where more acolytes were waiting for her with Atlantean armor.

The acolyte smiled. "My name is Kenya."

Calista smiled at her, "Thank you, Kenya."

The acolyte smiled with a small bow before walking out leaving Calista there to get suited up.

Calista was admiring her armor, just like all the Atlanteans it was lightweight but impenetrable, with intricate designs woven in with gems of multi colors. On her chest was a spider that resembled Scratch, who was giving his leg up in approval upon seeing it. She kissed his head. "Very fitting." Scratch moved himself so that he was underneath her shoulder armor, a pouch that she wondered if it was in all the armor or specifically designed for her. Everyone knew Scratch liked to ride on her shoulder, whatever the reason it worked perfectly for her.

She smiled as she saw she had a sword in her scabbard and there was also a shield with the Atlantean crest on it, a never ending circle with Atlantean symbols engraved within the lines of the spiral. Inside the circle two pieces of wheat crossed at the bottom while above them was a perfect replica of a sundial. She knew the writing in the circle spoke of Atlantis being the most advanced civilization and their pride in that. The Greeks were always looking for the pleasures of the here and now, while Atlanteans always looked forward. Another reason she knew Zeus had been so enthralled with her home.

"Speak of the devil," Calista murmured to herself as Zeus approached her. Behind him she could see the other Greek gods and goddesses gearing up for battle. Athena was there in full armor while Artemis and her maidens were practicing with their bows and arrows. The biggest shock to her was seeing Ares there with Discord, their armor showed her bloodlust, horns on their helmets while bones outlined their shields to show off their conquests.

"Granddaughter," Zeus acknowledged her, he laughed when she raised a brow at his greeting. "Forgive an old god, some habits are hard to break."

Calista nodded at him as he stood there in his armor, silver bands across his chest with golden lightning bolts, a belt of gold around his waist with red fabric hanging to his knees right above the top of his golden boots. While the Atlanteans and their armor covered more of their skin and all the vital areas, Zeus, with several of the other Greeks and many of the Ancients' Champions that had joined their cause, showed more skin than armor.

There was a female Champion whose skin was orange with green markings as if tattooed onto her, her hair was a darker green than her skin and weaved into her scalp, curling up on the top in the back to form the tip of a wave. She was creating orange symbols in the air with her hands, then would move them around, staring at them intently as if they were speaking to her. Of course, there was a chance they were.

There was a male who could be mistaken as a statue if he stood still, his skin gray and hard as stone. Even the breeches he wore looked as if they were carved from stone. As he moved, the ground moved with him. Calista watched as Hephaestus approached him and they started talking.

It was amazing for her to see everyone together here in Atlantis, the civilization that fell beneath the waters from Ares curse. Atlanteans, Greeks, and the Champions from the stars. This might work, the Ancients may be gods from the Stars but surely with two pantheons and these Champions, the odds had to be on their side.

She looked over at Zeus who was watching her closely. "I have one question for you."

Zeus nodded for her to proceed.

"Why?"

CHAPTER 17

Zeus frowned at her, "Why?"

"Yes, why." Calista looked at him. "Why are you guys joining in this battle? It isn't in your best interest. This has nothing to do with Greece." Even though Kenya spoke about why the Greeks were fighting alongside them, she wanted to hear it from Zeus himself.

Zeus took an uncharacteristically deep breath before responding, "Long ago, I stood by when Ares made a deal with the Gods from the Stars. I knew it was wrong, but it didn't affect Greece, so I turned my back on what my son was doing and lost a great ally that day." Zeus lifted his hand as if to gently touch her cheek but at her flinch, he pulled back with a sigh. "I tried to make amends by protecting you as much as I could." When she snorted his head nodded in acknowledgment. "I admit it wasn't much. I'd like to rectify my mistake and so we'll join you and your family in this battle."

"There is a chance none of us will survive this battle," Calista told him.

Zeus lifted a shoulder. "Then I'll pay the price for my mistake."

Calista stared at him, not sure what to say, that

wasn't what she expected. Neither the gods nor the goddesses of Greece were known for being selfless.

"Did I finally leave you speechless, granddaughter?" Zeus sounded amused.

"You could say that." She looked at him. "I won't say thank you."

Zeus chuckled. "I didn't expect you to."

Calista nodded and walked past him, not sure what to say or how to feel at this point. So much happened in her life and when it came to trusting someone, that wasn't her specialty. Growing up she had always yearned for any affection, but getting knocked down so much had hardened her heart. Even being with her parents and feeling the love they have shown her hadn't been enough to soften it.

Calista moved through the paths between the temples, heading towards where her parents were getting ready to meet the Ancients when they came. Within a week's time, many had gathered in Atlantis for this war. Atlantis was immense in size but this battle was shaping up to become larger than any battle Calista had seen and considering she grew up as Ares' daughter, that was saying a lot. Speaking of Ares, she saw him standing there with Discord and Strife. She moved off the path to stand in front of him.

Ares glared down at her. "What do you want, bug?" He glared at her while Discord and Strife snickered.

"If you don't want to be here then why are you?" Calista asked him.

Ares snorted. "Not for your sake, I assure you."

"You can thank Zeus for us being here, otherwise we would let the Ancients destroy all of you." Discord sneered at her, but she just ignored her, keeping her attention on Ares, who didn't look at all happy to have her attention on him.

"What favor did you do for the Ancients to get them to curse Atlantis?" Calista asked Ares, who tilted his head as he watched her, pausing before he answered.

"Not that it is any of your business but I was asked to make sure you lived but most importantly there was someone they wanted to be detained," Ares shrugged. "The Siren was easy, it was putting up with you on a daily basis that was hard to swallow."

Calista ignored the jab at her, she had heard those and worse ones during her life with Ares. But the comment about the Siren had her attention, "The Siren in the caves on Ithaca?"

Ares just smiled.

"You can't possibly be the one who imprisoned her there," Calista told him.

"What makes you say that?" he asked her.

"The runes that imprison her aren't Greek," Calista informed him, enjoying watching his eyes narrow at her.

He shrugged. "The Ancients didn't say I had to be the one to imprison her, just that I had to get the job done." His cruel smile showed his pride in that answer.

"In other words, get someone else to do your dirty work for you." Calista rolled her eyes at him.

Ares narrowed his eyes on her. "He was compensated for his services, I promise you that. Between the two of us I can promise you he got the better end of it."

"All you care about is what benefits you." Calista walked away from him, not wanting to hear any more. She had to listen to how great he thought he was most of her life, right now she just needed to figure out a way to defeat the Ancients before they destroyed all that she loved.

"Uncle." She turned when she heard Shaylane's happy words, Shaylane was smiling and hugging Alastor. She stopped right there as Brax glowered at Alastor, who was smiling at Shaylane.

"Uncle?" She looked between the three of them, confused.

"He's my brother," Brax spat out, still glowering. "Not that the fact mattered to him all those years ago."

"Father." Shaylane placed her hand on his arm. "We have discussed this, he had a part to play just as everyone else. Now is the time for forgiveness, we are joining together to battle a common enemy."

"Yes, brother." Alastor grinned that unhinged grin of his. "Let's put the past where it belongs and take down the infidels so we can drink, sing and be merry tonight."

"You betrayed us all to those infidels for your own selfish reasons," Brax told him tightly. If not for Shaylane standing between them, Calista was sure there might have been a fight, but Shaylane refused to budge.

"Enough, Father," she told him and Brax grudgingly backed back down.

An uncle must betray his family... Calista stopped and stared at Alastor but he didn't even look her way.

The runes that held the siren in that cave was Atlantean, she was sure of that. No other Atlantean would help Ares, but what could Ares give Alastor?

"It's time!"

Calista jerked around hearing the bellow from Stratos as he stood beside her grandparents and parents. She shimmered to her parents' side where Solen, Draken, Rikar, and Zeus stood with Hera.

There before them stood Lux, Loom, Lore, and Lars with several other silver Ancients, along with the Champions that were still loyal to them. Champions of all sizes, colors and powers. Lux moved forward towards them, Loom following a step behind. His voice was the same monotone as before, the same as all the Ancients. "Are you ready to come with us, Calista? It is the only way to save the ones you love." His threat was clear.

Her father stepped forward. "She isn't going anywhere with you."

Lux raised a brow at him. "Are you foolish enough to believe you can actually defeat us? Many have tried and failed." He looked out over the Champions that once served him and were now standing there on the side of the Atlanteans until his eyes rested on Solen. "You're making a grave mistake, Hunter."

"No, for once I'm making the right choice," Solen told them. "Your reign of tyranny is coming to an end."

Lore moved forward with an aggressive expression but Lux held up a hand, his face still impassive as always. "Hold." Lore stilled but his gaze still watched Solen. Lux turned his attention back to Solen. "Our reign of tyranny? Didn't we provide everything for you? We provided you with a home and a family, and you call us tyrants for that?"

"You took me from my home as well as the others." Solen turned to the other Champions who were still standing behind the Ancients. "None of you owe them anything either, you can stand against them as well, get your life back."

Lux clapped his hands slowly. "Bravo, Hunter, such an impassioned plea, but they understand the importance of loyalty. Something you need to be taught." He looked out over at the gods until his eyes landed on Calista. "All of you." He raised a hand and the Ancients moved back while their Champions rushed forward.

A Champion with a double-bladed scythe started forward twirling his blade so fast you couldn't see the beginning nor the end of the blade. His face was encased in a blue crystal diamond shaped mask with a golden frame around it, golden arches over his head and his body encased in complete brown leather armor. Atmos moved forward towards the Champion with his own blade held tightly in his grasp. Sparks flew as blade met blade.

Athena battled a Champion in full metal armor with a glowing silver blade, spear meeting blade as the Champion tried to sidestep her and striking Athena's side, right under her armor. She let out a shriek before bringing her shield down on the Champion's back.

Draken and Rikar were battling two Champions who were obviously twins, either that or one who could make duplicates of itself. She couldn't tell if it was male or female as there was no indication of either. They were purple in color, their skin resembling a cosmic night sky, bracers adorned both wrists while the only other armor they wore was a golden headpiece with a purple gem, a purple and black cloth around their waist, boots and an intricately designed golden chest piece with an unusual centerpiece of purple, black and gold.

They were holding their own with the creatures until both creatures brandished mighty purple wings that started to beat down on the brothers, sending wave after wave of purple mist that started to suffocate the brothers.

"NO!" Calista shouted running towards them, her

intent to distract the twins long enough for the brothers to regain their ground. She had crouched to leapt up on one of the twin's backs when she was knocked out of the air onto the ground where she rolled then flipped so that she was poised crouched on the ground, facing her enemy.

There stood a Champion before her that embodied the word … evil. Full body black armor, hard edges and a black shield over the face. Darkness followed his each move, black smoke curling in the Champion's hands. She looked over at the brothers but she needn't have feared, they had shifted to dragons and were now in the process of taking down the twins by their wings. The purple haze did not affect them in their dragon forms.

Solen battled a muscular Champion who was bringing down his sword on Solen's shield. Her mother and Athena battled a group of Champions that could multiply themselves, her eyes narrowed when she saw Ares join in, bringing his sword down on one of the duplicates, it disappeared only to reappear only feet away.

A movement in front of her had her leaping back just as a dark cloud moved past her face barely missing her, although a small lock of her hair glided through the dark cloud. The hair turned from blond to dead black and slowly falling to the ground. Calista manipulated the air around the Champion to form a crystal cell to contain him, but to her horror the Champion walked right through as if it were nothing.

"That's not good," Calista looked around her as the battle started to turn against the Champions, well all except hers, she thought as she turned around just in time to see another dark cloud coming her way. She ducked and rolled, sending an energy bolt along the ground to the metal boots the Champion wore.

She watched as the bolt ran up his leg branching off to both legs, the chest, arms and the helmet sparking with each movement sending the dark Champion to the ground, twitching. Standing, she looked around the battleground feeling more confident, the Champions were falling to the might of the gods and other Champions; they were winning.

She felt a movement on her shoulder as Scratch leapt out to join the fun, when she saw a nimble Champion dressed in yellow with long lanky arms and spears for hands jump out of the way of the spider. She was about to transport the Champion elsewhere and out of the way of her spider when the Champion shocked her by running away with a scream that was so high pitched it couldn't come from anyone human.

She laughed as Scratch turned back to her with a proud little grin, "Don't get too cocky there, little troublemaker." When he disappeared she sent him a message, "Be careful Scratch, immortal doesn't mean you can't be harmed." She could hear the eye roll from her best friend.

She moved across the battlefield creating quicksand

beneath the legs of Champions so that they were encased in the ground below. Dodging blades, axes and many other forms of weapons that were either metal or enhanced by many sorts of powers wielded by the Champions.

She kept her attention on the many Champions they battled but also on Scratch, who at this moment crawled into the armor of a Champion, causing enough of a distraction to give her father the advantage. With a wave of his hand, the armor the Champion was wearing turned into thousands of spiders, Scratch jumped down, insulted. sending some choice words her father's way. He needed no help from fake spiders, was the nice way of paraphrasing his words.

"Let's finish this!" Tylaos shouted holding up his staff with Atlantean markings running along the shaft and the circular globe on top with many images floating around showing the advancement of time. Many that were foreign to Calista and some not so foreign.

CHAPTER 18

"I agree, it's time to finish this!"

Calista turned to see Lux standing there with at least several dozen other Ancients. She frowned, even with that many Ancients they were still outnumbered and their Champions had either been defeated or were being pushed back.

"Your Champions are defeated, Lux," Tylaos spoke. "Leave now and never darken our door again. We will let you leave in peace, but only if you leave now."

Lux's expression never wavered, never changed, stayed the neutral look with no expression as he responded, "You think you've beaten us?"

Malis stepped forward putting her armored foot on the top of the scaly back of the Champion that she had just defeated. "Your Champions are defeated. We've won and you've lost. You'll not get our daughter, Ancient one."

Lux barely acknowledged her as he stepped forward with the others moving in exact sync with him. When he spoke, his words echoed all around them, "You think we are powerless without our Champions? They are nothing more than tools in our arsenal, expendable tools that are easily replaced once they serve their purpose."

Calista couldn't help but glance towards Solen at Lux's words, she could see the tightening around his mouth and she felt a rush of anger at how easily Lux could dismiss everyone who was loyal to him. She turned her glare towards Lux. "If they are so easily expendable then why even bother to take them from their homes? Why go out of your way to lie, cheat and bully them to get your way? I think you do need them, you just don't like to admit it."

"Gods always create Champions to do the work that is beneath them. The Champions should be proud to serve their purpose to higher beings. That is their purpose, while our purpose is to remind them exactly what they are," Lux told her in his haughty manner.

"And what is that?" Calista had a feeling she wouldn't like the response and she was correct.

"Slaves to the gods they serve. Their wants nor their needs no longer matter, only their servitude and once that is no longer needed, then neither are they." Lux reached out to one of the Champions who had stayed loyal to them, one who was retreating from the battle. As soon as Lux's silver hand touched the Champion's coarse black skin, the color started to fade and the Champion looked up at Lux, his eyes wide as he started to gasp out for breath. "Let me correct that, they are no longer needed, so they must give their masters all they have left... their powers." As he spoke, the Champion fell to the ground, his skin now translucent and his eyes lifeless. In Lux's hand a lava ball started to form, he looked up and sent the lava ball straight for Solen, who was so shocked from what he was seeing that he never dodged, the ball hit him squarely in the chest.

"Noooo!" Calista screamed, rushing to Solen's side as he stumbled before falling to his knees and crumbling to the ground. She reached him and was able to hold him before he hit the ground. She stared into his pained eyes, looking at the charred mark in his chest, her eyes filling with tears as she glared at Lux. "How could you?"

"I already told you," Lux stated. "They are expendable once their services have been fulfilled."

She watched as several of the other Ancients moved forward, touching the nearest Champion to them. As the Atlanteans, Greeks and Champions who fought at their side watched, these Champions all fell like their comrades and each Ancient now contained their power.

Lux moved towards her. "If you refuse to fulfill your destiny as one of our Champions then taking your powers will have to suffice; either way, your powers will become ours."

"You're no gods," Calista spat at him as he approached, refusing to leave Solen's side. "You're nothing more than monsters."

Not pausing his steps, the Ancients behind still moving in sync as Champions rushed to get out of their path, Lux continued speaking to her. "Your first mistake was in assuming the Champions were our only defense, don't make a second one. I'll only give you one more chance to come with us before we take everything you love. We will make sure you will watch as your loved ones are drained before we put you out of your misery. Come with us now and we will let them live, that is our final offer." Lux's usually calm voice started to show the emotion of his aggravation with the situation.

"Spider," Solen's weak voice reached her as his hand wrapped weakly around her wrist. "You need to run."

"I can't leave you," Calista told him tearfully as she could feel Lux getting closer.

Solen gave her a weak smile. "You can't let them touch you, if you do, all that has happened here will be for nothing. Don't let that happen."

Calista felt a tear fall down her cheek and watched as it rolled down, splashing onto his cheek. "I'm so sorry, Solen."

He shook his head. "Don't be sorry, Spider, just show them the true goddess you are." He pulled her head down and pressed a gentle kiss to her lips before closing his eyes, his head falling back.

Calista could barely contain the grief-stricken sob that escaped her, she laid his body down then looked up at the Ancient who was almost upon her. "You won't get what you want, that I promise you." Her words were full of her tears.

"We shall see." Lux moved forward, but Calista let her manipulative powers loose as she started to put up barriers in front of the Ancients.

Each Ancient stopped as they hit the invisible wall, then held out their hands and absorbed the energy inside themselves. With each absorption, Calista felt as if they were draining a part of her. She moved back, her breathing labored as she felt weaker. The Ancients watching her started to smile. She thought they looked creepy when they didn't smile, they looked even worse when they did.

"Don't let them touch you!" she shouted out to everyone.

"Easier said than done," Draken shouted to her, moving to avoid an Ancient.

"Just imagine them as your latest conquest," she shot back, knowing how the brothers never dated the same woman twice.

Rikar grinned looking at his brother. "That could work."

"Don't encourage her," his brother shot back, moving to avoid letting one of the Ancients touch him. "So, if we can't let them touch us, how do we fight back?"

Zeus sent lightning bolts down onto the Ancients, some were knocked down and injured but they would quickly rebound and, placing their hands on the still sparking bolts, they absorbed them into themselves. Calista looked over at Zeus, who looked as if he grew weaker with each absorption, just like she had.

"Powers aren't working either," she told everyone, her stomach starting to plummet with the realization that they had no defense against these gods from the skies.

A movement out of her side was her only warning that Lux had finally reached her, she jerked away just as he was about to touch her. Scratch jumped onto the Ancient in defense of his mistress before she could stop him.

"Scratch! Stop!" She was too late, Lux grabbed Scratch who squirmed in his hand for only seconds before going limp. Lux tossed him aside like a piece of garbage, Calista felt her anger and grief collide within her as she let out a blood-curdling scream, launching herself at Lux without thinking.

Shouts from her parents and the others seemed as if they had come from a distance. Her vision was red and all she could see was the visions of Solen and Scratch in front of her, everyone she cared for was here and their lives were in jeopardy. All because of her.

She hit Lux with her shoulder and they went tumbling, landing with her on her back and Lux looking down at her in triumph. She truly liked them better when they had no expressions. She could see her life before her eyes as Lux placed his hand on her armored chest, she waited for the draining feeling of losing her powers, of losing herself.

But that feeling didn't come, Lux frowned then he

saw her bare neck, moving with each breath she took and no armor to protect it. He moved to wrap his around her neck and she realized even their powers had limitations. Raising her armored arm she used her fore-arm to knock him back off of her so she could roll away. "They can't drain us through the armor, just don't let them touch your bare skin."

"That leaves most of the Greeks out," Rikar quipped, earning glares from the Greek gods and Goddesses while Malis sent a reproving glance his way.

"This isn't the time, Rikar," she told him, but he only winked at her. She tried to hold back the smile but it broke through. "He is right though, those with limited armor stand back while those of us with more armor can advance. The ones with limited armor can use their powers to help those with more armor, just be careful in using your powers against the Ancients."

They did have an advantage now but not enough of one to keep the advantage they had when fighting the Champions. The Ancients still had the powers of the Champions they had already drained.

Athena was able to join the Atlanteans in their battle and even though Alastor spent the last several decades being a Greek god, he was wearing the Atlantean armor, which meant he was very well covered.

Calista was facing off with Lux, who was still trying to drain her power from her. She could feel the heat of the lava beneath her feet as Lux called it forward from the ground. Calista flipped backwards just as the ground started to flow with the molten rock. "You missed!" Calista said as she rose but Lux was no longer standing there on the other side of the lava pool.

"Did I?" His mocking voice came from behind her, she twirled around to see him standing barely inches from her. "You think one Guardian is the only one I have drained? I have drained many in my lifetime and it takes several lifetimes before their powers disappear."

Calista raised her sword to bring it down on Lux, who once again disappeared, only to reappear behind her once again. She was ready for him this time, turning to bring her sword down on his neck only to watch as it shattered upon impact.

"As I said, I have absorbed many powers and I always make sure to keep a fresh stash just in case." As he spoke he reached out with his hardened hand to grip her throat and raise her off the ground. "Last chance, Calista. Join us now or become another expendable."

Calista clawed at his hand, feeling the air being cut off by his grip but not feeling a draining sensation. Her confusion must have shown in her face for Lux explained. "While I am using this power to armor my skin, I'm unable to absorb your power, but as it fades," she could see his skin's hardness start to fade starting at the top of his head and moving down as he said that, "I will once again be able to absorb your power. You have until it reaches my hand to make your choice."

She tried to shimmer from his grasp but he only shook his head. "No shimmering away for you, another power of mine is to neutralize powers, and it is an effective one. You were foolish to believe we were powerless because we didn't show off our powers. You should always learn about your enemies before you go into battle with them, didn't you learn anything from growing up with Ares?"

She kept trying to squirm out of his grasp as she watched the hardness on his skin fading closer to his hand that held her. "Ares wasn't much of a teacher," she managed to gasp out.

Lux nodded his head slightly, "I can see his ego and pompous manner getting in the way." He looked down at his arm that was no longer hardened, watching as the hardness started disappearing from his wrist. "Your time is running out, better choose quickly."

"Go to Hades," she spat out at him, refusing to be a slave to him or any of the Ancients.

"You first," he told her as the hardness disappeared from his hand and Calista started to fall, her power and energy slowly draining from her. "Just remember, you were given the option, but don't worry, I won't drain you completely just yet. I promised I would let you watch your loved ones be drained completely first."

The edges of her vision started to grow dim, she could see her family fighting alongside the Greeks and Champions. She felt great despair welling up inside her as she realized the battle was about to be lost to these tyrants.

"Back off of her!"

Calista barely heard the angry growl as she was suddenly thrown to the ground gasping for air and holding her throat trying to breath. She looked and saw Alastor raising a battle axe in the air to bring it down on Lux, who blasted his armored chest with a lava ball. Alastor, unlike Solen, was a god so it didn't kill him but it did knock him back on his ass. Lux reached for him and grabbed his bare neck. "You have troubled me for the last time."

Calista tried to jump up to save him as he had saved her, but her strength was just beginning to rebound, and not as quickly as she had hoped.

Alastor looked at her with no fear in his eyes, only acceptance. "This is my penance, princess, now you must run and free the goddess if you want to save your family."

"I don't know where she is," Calista said, feeling tears of frustration fill her eyes. Why did she have to be the one to save a goddess she had never met?

"Yes you do, I gave Ares the imprisoning spell to secure me a place in the Greek Pantheon, a spell only you can break." He told her as his voice grew weaker. "Go now!" His final words were barely a whisper before the life drained out of his eyes and the Ancients killed a god.

Lux turned to her. "I know I promised you could

watch your loved ones be drained, but I have found that I have lost my patience. Time for this to be over."

Calista looked up at him, realizing what Alastor and the prophecy meant. "You're right, it is." With those words she shimmered from Atlantis before Lux could get close enough to neutralize her powers. The last thing she heard were the grunts of the battle and Lux's frustrated scream of denial.

CHAPTER 19

The water looked so calm around the island of Crete, no evidence that deep below the surface there was a war being fought right now. How she hated leaving them. "This better work," she muttered looking around.

"Talking to yourself is a sign of insanity, so they say," came a singsong voice from the nearby cave. A voice remembered from her childhood, the imprisoned siren.

Calista moved closer to the cave and just like when she was younger the glyphs lit up, every other one tilted. Then from the darkness of the cave came the gentle face of the silver haired Siren she met so long ago. "Hello again."

"Hi." Calista knew it sounded trite but she didn't know what to do as she stood there looking at the Siren's face staring back at her quietly. "Ummm, are you the imprisoned goddess?" Okay, that didn't sound any better.

But the Siren smiled at her and nodded. "I've waited a long time for you to come into your power and release me; my name is Aesis."

"Hello, Aesis." Calista smiled at her then looked at the runes along the outside entrance to the cave that created a barrier no one could pass. "So, since you are the goddess who must be freed then I must be the goddess that was awakened. Probably when I discovered my powers."

"Probably," Aesis said, smiling as she watched as Calista started to put everything together.

"Saying I must manipulate the odds has to do with my powers of manipulation and the runes that are odd and don't match with the others," she continued while Aesis watched silently. Calista could see approval in the eyes of the Siren. Goddess, she silently amended. Calista put her hand on the first rune that was tilted and focused her power on that rune to manipulate it so that it was correctly positioned. As soon as the rune was righted, it glowed brightly as well as the two connecting runes.

Calista placed her palm on the next tilted rune, righting the rune and creating another connection as the next two runes lit up. Soon she was down to the last two runes with only one tilted, just as she was about to place her hand on the tilted one she heard a movement from behind her.

There standing just outside of the cave glancing at the imprisoned siren warily was Loom, the female Ancient. "You mustn't release that thing."

"Is that actual fear I hear in your voice?" Calista asked, honestly curious. She heard the monotone voice as well as the mockery and aggression from earlier, but this was the first time she heard fear.

"You don't understand, if you release that thing then you doom us all, including you and your family," Loom tried to reason with her.

"Except that, according to your leader, my family is already doomed," Calista reminded her. "So, I don't see what the difference is for us." During the exchange, the Siren stayed silent but her gaze never wavered from the Ancient, not once did she glance Calista's way since the Ancient showed up. Something that seemed to make Loom very uncomfortable.

"The difference is you have a chance with us but with her you're looking at total annihilation of your world," Loom told her. "Would serving us be so bad? We would provide you a home, food and a purpose."

Calista stared at her. "Are you even listening to yourself? You're trying to make slavery sound appealing."

"That is what they do." Shaylane moved from the shadows. "First they try to convince you to join them as their slave and if you don't fall for their deception then they fall back on intimidation. If that doesn't work then comes the threats of annihilation, and finally they act on those threats."

"Shaylane!" Calista frowned at her, her attention moving from the Ancient one to Shaylane. "What are you doing here?"

"I knew Loom would try to stop you from releasing the goddess," Shaylane told her. "I might not be as powerful as my mother with my visions, but I'm able to see far enough to know I was needed here."

"Needed here? For what?" Calista questioned her.

A blur to her left had her turning to see Loom lunge for her, she held up her arms to protect her but the attack never came. Putting her arms down she gasped when she saw Loom holding Shaylane by her throat. "If you want your friend to live, you will undo what you have started."

Calista silently cursed herself for letting Loom distract her, she looked into Shaylane's eyes but instead of fear there all she saw was confidence. Shaylane gave a small nod to her, as much of a nod as she could give with Loom's fingers tightening on her throat. Calista could see Shaylane's skin growing translucent from Loom's touch.

"If you don't act quickly, there won't be much of your friend left." Loom's voice turned cold.

Calista turned and touched the last glyph, righting it quickly so the entire line of glyphs glowed brightly releasing Aesis from her prison.

Loom released Shaylane, letting out a petrified shriek as Aesis reached for her before she was able to disappear. Shaylane fell to the ground, scrambling backwards as she stared.

Aesis stared into Loom's wide eyes. "Taste me."

Loom's eyes started to bulge and her silver skin started to smoke as her shriek became a garbled moan as Aesis released all that was left of Loom, letting the husk crumble to the ground in a heap of dull silver.

Calista stared at her. "How did you do that? We couldn't even touch them without losing our powers."

Aesis smiled at her. "We are poison to them; long ago when they came to our world attempting to drain us and our powers they discovered that to their horror. You see, these so-called Ancients used to travel the stars looking for slaves to take back to their world. They would take what power they wanted and those who didn't have what they wanted, they would take them as their slaves, until they came upon our world." Aesis looked back down at the pile at her feet. "They called themselves gods and who knows, maybe they are in their world, but in mine they were nothing more than parasites. When they attempted to drain one of our people, they discovered we were poisonous to them. They tried to run but we followed and destroyed all those we could."

She turned to look at Calista and Shaylane. "There were some that escaped our wrath, those that escaped started to enslave others to fight their battles for them. No longer would they drain the most powerful and take the weaker ones for slaves, unless they couldn't get what they wanted. They were able to amass an army and they captured me, holding me hostage to keep my people at bay. My people have been waiting for the one to come along and free me."

"You created the prophecy?" Calista frowned.

Aesis nodded. "And you answered. Now let's go save

your family and loved ones." Tilting her head back she let out the most beautiful sound Calista had ever heard, not even Apollo with his lyre could compare.

All around them shooting stars fell from the sky, it was a beautiful sight. These stars fell into the water, leaving shining waves in their wake. Aesis smiled at them both. "Let's go, we both need to be reunited with our families."

Calista wasn't sure what to expect when they arrived in Atlantis but the sight that greeted them gave her a mixture of apprehension and one of thankfulness. Piles of dull, silver husks littered the floor of Atlantis, while the few Champions left that had fought against them were in chains.

Standing around were beings that looked as if they were made of pure light, as they watched, the glow around the beings began to fade away, leaving humanoid looking beings with darkened skin. Aesis moved from Calista's side rushing into the arms of the tallest male standing over a silver husk. "Father!" Calista watched, smiling as they embraced.

"Shaylane!" Calista turned to see Brax rush to embrace his daughter. She had to admit she was happy to see that he was okay, for Shaylane to come all this way and her father to perish in a battle protecting Calista, the guilt would've been too much.

"Calista!" Turning Calista smiled as her own parents rushed to embrace her in their arms.

"Good to see the princess is still in one piece." She turned to see Rikar and Draken smiling at her. She rushed to hug them both. She looked around then turned back to her parents and asked the question she hated to ask, "Scratch?"

Their sad little shakes of their heads brought tears to her eyes, her one true best friend who had never left her side. Her father pulled her into his arms and held her tightly. "I'm sorry, my daughter. We couldn't save him."

She leaned into him and let the tears flow. It wasn't fair, she had just lost her best friend. She lifted her head as she thought about something else and looked at her father. "Solen?" Did she lose him, too?

"He's waiting for you in Brine's temple," came Rowena's soft voice from behind her.

Calista looked at her parents and the brothers, who all nodded. She rushed to the entrance of Brine's temple where the acolytes nodded to her with respect as she entered. There, laying on one of the beds of sheepskins, was Solen with wraps around his chest. He looked up as she entered and smiled at her. She rushed to his side and hugged him, jerking back at his painful groan. "Sorry," she said, moving back in regret.

He put his hand on her leg to hold her still. "No worries, Spider. To get a greeting like that from you, I'll take the pain."

She gave a nervous laugh, staying there smiling down at him. "I'm just happy to see you alive."

"Worried about me, were you?" He gave a painful smile.

"Yes, I was," she admitted, then brushed a lock of hair behind her ear. "I like having you around."

"I like being around," he admitted. "So, you managed to save us all." It wasn't a question but still she nodded, telling him how she freed Aesis and how she brought her people to stop the Ancients. As she spoke, she saw his eyelids grow heavy.

"He needs rest." She looked up and saw Brine standing there, no longer in her armor but in Atlantean finery as she smiled at her niece. "And you need to join your parents and grandparents as we thank our saviors."

Calista looked down at the sleeping Solen then back at her aunt and nodded as she rose.

The celebration in Atlantis lasted several days and several nights. The Greek gods and goddesses joined the celebration as well as Aesis and her people. They were actual gods of the stars who weren't tied to any world and was why they were able to chase down the Ancients world to world.

Their true selves were the beings of light they first saw, but as gods they were also able to change their form. Although when they are corporeal they weren't as strong, and that was when Aesis was captured by a Champion of the Ancients.

Gark, the father of Aesis, stood up with a goblet of wine. "Thanks to our new friends, our daughter has been returned to us. We owe you a great debt."

Tylaos stood as well with his goblet. "No debt. You saved my family as well, I will take your friendship over a debt." He held out his hand to Gark, who clasped the hand in agreement.

"You have it!" Gark declared and the whole room erupted in cheers. Calista looked over at Solen, who was back in his leather breeches, and long leather cloak he called a coat. He never looked better in her eyes.

She stood up and headed out into the gardens of her grandparents' temple; the battle was over and now she just wanted a moment alone. The garden managed to escape the damage from the battle that raged only days ago, many places were still healing from the damage. Rowena had been using her magic to repair much of the damage done as well the other Gods and goddesses, but per her grandparents, tonight was a night of celebration.

She could feel the presence of another god in the garden, she moved slightly to see Zeus walking towards her. She no longer hated him as she had before but she couldn't say she trusted him either. A truce had been called between the Atlanteans and Greeks, but she knew to be careful even with the truce.

"Zeus." She acknowledged him with a nod as he reached her.

"May I?" He motioned to the space on the bench next to her.

She gave a shrug. "I don't see why not."

He sat down next to her. "I'm sorry to hear about Scratch," he started to say, but she held up her hand.

"Don't!" She didn't want to hear generic placates from him about Scratch, and refused to let him tarnish the memory of her best friend.

"I know I messed up, I should've done more and I also know there is nothing I can do to make up for my mistakes," he said to her.

"If you expect me to refute that—" she started to say but he shook his head.

"I don't." He sighed. "I know this won't make up for everything but I hope it will at least give you a sense of peace."

"This?" Calista looked over at him.

He held up a necklace, Calista took the necklace and there encased in a teardrop crystal was Scratch. She frowned at him. "What is this?"

"I couldn't bring him back, even though the Ancient hadn't drained all of his essence, so I encased him in this protective crystal where he will stay in a state of deep sleep until a cure can be found for him."

Calista stared down at the necklace, then back at Zeus, with tears in her eyes she flung her arms around him and hugged him. For the first time that she could re-member, she felt Zeus' arms wrap around her and hold her to him.

"Thank you, Grandfather," she told him and meant it.

CHAPTER 20

"Must you leave?" Calista sat on a bench inside her newly built temple talking with Solen. It had been several weeks after the celebration and Solen was completely healed.

"There are still more Champions enslaved by the remaining Ancients," Solen told her. "They are my friends and I need to free them."

"I could go with you," she said, rising to stand with him, reaching for his hands that clasped hers.

"I wish you could, Spider, but you can't just leave your family after finding them. I would never ask that of you," he told her, leaning his forehead on hers.

"I'm offering it." She looked up into his eyes.

"I don't know how long I'll be gone, I don't know how far into the stars I'll have to go to rescue all those who have been torn from their worlds by the Ancients," he told her. "I can't ask that of you, I won't ask that of you. You would end up hating me, and I won't have that either."

She looked at him, hating this feeling of loss, but she couldn't deny that she didn't like the idea of leaving her family after finally finding them. She also didn't like the idea of losing Solen after finding him. "Come back to me?"

"When we have freed all the Champions enslaved by the remaining Ancients and ensured that there will be no more enslaved," he promised her.

"We?" She looked up at him.

"I'll make sure no harm comes to him for you," Aesis spoke from the doorway.

She looked over at Aesis. "You're going as well?"

Aesis nodded. "Yes, as well as several others of my people."

"Not to mention the Champions who survived the battle," Solen told her. "I won't be doing this by myself."

Calista smiled at him. "At least I won't have to worry about you being alone. Just worry about you forgetting about me."

Solen lifted her face and kissed her softly before speaking against her lips, "That, Spider, will never happen."

20th century

Calista leaned against the railing as she looked out over the ocean in front of her. Today was the anniversary of that fateful day when she lost Scratch and Solen. Her fingers reached for the necklace that she never took off, holding the teardrop crystal that encased Scratch. During the years since that battle, she never left Atlantis, never ventured out as the world above them continued to change. It had taken Draken and his never ending badgering to get her to venture from her home and temple to explore the new world.

She always returned home to celebrate their victory, mostly in the hopes of seeing if Solen had finally returned, only to be disappointed. It had been many years now since she had returned home, after all her exploring of the world and all the many places, she had come to call this place called Georgia home. She had finally accepted that Solen wasn't coming home and created a life here for herself. She was a detective at the local law enforcement, standing up for those who couldn't stand up for themselves.

She knew back home they would be celebrating; you never stop celebrating freedom. Which was another reason she had come to call this place home, this land called America. When she had finally decided to let go of Solen, to accept he had either perished out there in the stars or wasn't coming home, she felt a peace wash over her that she had never felt. So to celebrate she had found a tattoo parlor and now sported a majestic phoenix that adorned her right ribs and hip.

"Your parents have been asking about you," came a familiar voice she hadn't heard in a long time.

Turning around she grinned at Rikar and Draken,

who stood only feet away from her. "How are they doing?"

"Doing well," Rikar told her as he moved closer. "Although they're missing their little girl. Cael wanted me to make sure to let you know."

A sigh escaped her lips. "I miss them too," she admitted.

"So, why not go home, then?" Draken asked her as he moved to the other side of her, his hip leaning on the railing.

She frowned up at him. "You two were the ones who basically kicked me out of my home and told me to find a life in the new world, which I've done," she finished, crossing her arms.

Draken's eyes darkened as his brow furrowed, "We didn't kick you out, we were just tired of watching you mope after that fool who hadn't returned." Solen had become a sore spot with Draken, who felt as if he had betrayed her by not returning.

Her shoulder lifted. "Tomatoes, tomahtoes."

When Draken didn't look one bit amused, she let out a small laugh. "I've truly missed you two."

Rikar lifted her in his arms and swung her around. "We've missed you as well. No one to tease."

"Since when?" She laughed as he put her down and Draken wrapped her in his arms, placing a kiss on her head before releasing her.

"Well, no one as fun as you." Rikar winked at her.

She just gave a shake of her head, still smiling. "I'll come home when I'm ready, I promise."

"When will that be?" Draken asked, looking down at her, she still hated that.

She shrugged, moving back until she felt the railing at her back as she spoke, "I don't know but I do know it isn't time right now."

"What will you do?" Rikar asked her.

She looked at him with a half smile and told him simply, "Live."

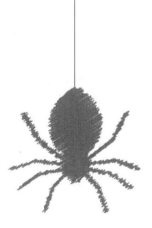

Made in the USA
Columbia, SC
28 August 2023